Caught Between Worlds

The story of three youths struggling to find identity in the challenges of a rugged environment, both human and natural.

Set in the late 1970s and truly timeless.

To Nick

who found his path between two worlds.

And to all others on their journey.

This book is a work of fiction. Names, characters, places and incidents are the product of the author's imagination or are used fictitiously. Any resemblance to actual events, locales, or persons, living and dead, is coincidental.

Published under the imprint of MJV Literary, London, United Kingdom.
Cover design by Maja Kopunovic.
Printed in the United States of America.

ISBN: 978-1-7370065-0-3

More about the author, his blog, and discussion forum can be found at:
https://www.lancepacker.com

Caught Between Worlds

Lance V. Packer

MJV

Chapters

1
Landing

Cal

Cal had just finished coiling up some extra dock line, tying his father's fishing boat to the wharf, when he thought he caught a distant droning sound. He glanced around him at the gray, breeze-rippled sea. The sky was overcast and heavy, but still cleared the tops of the stark tundra hills surrounding the town and harbor.

It was only the second day of decent weather they'd had in the entire month of August, and everyone in Biorka was sure that the RAA Goose would fly in today. It had made a couple of trips earlier in the month, bringing the weekly mail and ferrying out a few cannery workers.

But this day was going to be different: the new teachers would probably come today, having to beat the first fall storms, which would lock the town down tight for several weeks. After all, school was starting the first day of next week.

Cal Larson smiled slightly, and happily tossed the coil of line to the seiner's deck. As he climbed up the ladder which led to the top of the wharf, where the *Panof* was tied up, a voice called out:

"Hey, Cal!"

Cal looked up, and saw the stocky frame of his cousin and

best friend, Lawrence Carlson, striding toward him. "Hey, the Goose is coming," Lawrence grinned, broadly.

Cal tried to shrug off Lawrence's enthusiasm, but Lawrence was effusive. "I bet the teachers are on that one, eh?"

"Yeah, probably so."

"I wonder who we'll get this year to give a hard time to," Lawrence grinned. "Holy, that Jackson guy last year; we gave him a lot of trouble!"

Cal cast a glance at his cousin and allowed a thin smile. He was actually kind of curious himself to see what the plane would bring this year. Jackson was the target last year, and a good one at that.

As the two boys walked past the can-shop building, where massive machines were noisily sealing long lines of cans filled with salmon, a gust of wind caught them when it funneled past the cookhouse, making them side-step to regain their balance. With the gust, the rasping drone of the airplane was suddenly brought clearer.

Flying out on the Aleutian Islands chain of Alaska was tough—some of the toughest in the world, in fact, with the archipelago's sinuous, obscuring cloud banks, sudden, roaring williwaw winds, and a thousand miles of rough-hewn coastline and tossing sea.

Reeve Aleutian Airline had a published flight schedule, but that meant little to anyone out here; pilots flew only when it was reasonably safe, and even then they still hoped for the best. Passengers and waiting townspeople frequently glanced skyward while going through their daily routines, hoping for good weather and the familiar drone of the amphibious plane.

And, as if on cue, around the sharp promontory which formed the northwest end of Biorka Bay, would come the familiar, blue and white Grumman G-21 Goose. Flying low over the water, it truly looked like a heavy Canadian "Honker", with its ponderous white boat-belly hanging down, and pontoons suspended on both outboard sides of the engines, which were stuck in each wing. As ungainly as it seemed, it was well-suited to the environment and needs of the Aleutians.

After planing in upon the surface of the bay like a speedboat, the airplane settled heavily in the water—drenching spray pouring up over the cockpit windows—then idled up close to the beach.

Then, with fire and smoke belching from each engine, spray and beach debris whipped up behind it, the plane leaped for the beach; on its lowered wheels, it lurched and lumbered like a prehistoric amphibian, up the stony surface. With a quick acceleration of the port engine, and a sharp right rudder, the pilot spun the plane parallel with the beachline, blasting the bystanders with sand and spray.

All of a sudden the engines shut down, the plane rocked back into the sand, and silence once again rushed in to claim its natural right. A few seconds later, the rear door was flung open.

Cal had seen this miracle of machinery do its dance before, hundreds of times—just as all of the other townspeople had—but it still commanded his attention. Any event to break the monotony of life here was guaranteed a crowd, and a crowd was now gathering for this one.

The boardwalk along which Cal and Lawrence were

strolling was the main thoroughfare, from one part of the small town to another. Most of the houses were built along the grassy gravel beach ridge which formed the mile-long spit, reaching from the hills to the lagoon entrance, and the boardwalk ran the length of this ridge, between the houses and the beach. The boys went past the cannery office and the health clinic, which formed the last buildings of the cannery complex.

In front of them, Cal spotted a familiar head among a group of girls, ambling toward the landing spot on the beach. Lawrence was giving a rather long-winded account of how his Uncle Louis had got two fingers caught in a winch drum yesterday aboard his dad's boat, the *Korovin*, and nearly lost them, when Cal elbowed him in the ribs to make him shut up. Lawrence glanced over at Cal, caught the direction he was looking and fell silent. Catherine was among the girls, Lawrence noted—that must be it. Without another word, both boys shoved their hands a little deeper into their pants pockets and assumed a more swaggering gait. With an unconcerned air, their turned-down hip boots slapping noisily with each stride, they sauntered toward the knot of girls gathered just up from the landing spot, near Molly's store.

2
Landing

Catherine

Catherine Cheripanof noticed Cal as soon as the boys emerged from between the cannery buildings.

She had been on her way to buy some shampoo when she ran into Ruth Dudren and Alice Franks, hurrying to watch the plane land. They were her best friends, but she hadn't seen either of them for several days.

By the time Cal and Lawrence came over, three other younger girls had joined the group, and all were now busy sharing the latest gossip. Catherine said nothing to the group, but Ruth soon noticed that she wasn't listening very closely to Alice's story about her mother's latest boyfriend in Anchorage, and quickly caught the reason for her inattention. With a knowing smile, she gave Catherine a strong nudge with her elbow, which tilted her off balance.

"Hey, what'cha doin'?" Alice flashed a frown as Catherine fell against her to catch herself, then broke into smiles as she saw the cause of the disturbance approaching.

"Cathy, your lover's comin'!" one of the younger girls sang, in a tease. The other girls started giggling.

"I don't have any lover," Catherine said in mock anger,

trying to cover her smile.

"Don't act so dumb," Alice chided the younger girls, as their heads bobbed with stifled laughter. As the boys approached, the giggling died down and stopped.

Being the boldest, Alice spoke first: "Hi, Cal, Lawrence."

"Hi," both said together.

"Where you been this last week?" Lawrence asked.

"Oh, out Anchorage, visitin' my mom."

"How's she doin'?"

"Okay."

The roar of the plane landing on the beach took precedence for a moment, as it pelted the group with seaweed and sand. Out of habit, all bystanders turned their backs to the blast, and hunkered down in the protection of their flapping coats and jacket collars.

"Hi, Catherine," Cal muttered, as he straightened his shoulders and gave a tug at his fancy Greek fisherman's cap. Unlike their fathers, who wore the traditional knit watch-caps, most of the Biorka fishermen's sons wore the more stylish, braided-bill Greek caps. Cal bought his last spring, and it was now an inseparable part of him.

"Hi, Cal. How'd you do this trip out?" Catherine replied, referring to the last fishing trip of the *Panof*.

"Okay," Cal shrugged.

Lawrence blurted out: "Okay? You said you and your dad pulled in twenty-thousand dollars' worth yesterday alone!"

"Yeah, we did. It was okay." *Damn,* Cal thought, *can't Lawrence ever keep his mouth shut?*

"Hey, that's pretty good," Catherine encouraged.

"Might even keep him in booze for a week!" Lawrence interjected. This brought giggles and snickers from the girls.

Even Cal had to smile, shifting his weight to the other foot and glancing vacantly out to sea. Lawrence did pull funny ones sometimes, Cal had to admit to himself, as he looked back and picked up some furtive, coy glances from the other girls.

"Nah," Cal countered, "I'm going to get a new three-wheeler. It's coming from Anchorage this month." Cal paused and, looking out to sea for the invisible barge again, grumbled: "Shoulda been here by now."

"Lucky Catherine!" Ruth chided.

The group jostled each other as Cal and Catherine took some verbal teasing jabs, but both of them remained cool. Only Catherine flushed a little color.

By now, the orange and green mailbags were being thrown out of the front hatch of the Goose. Passengers were stepping out of the rear door, too, and all attention was focused there.

A local man got off first. He gave a quick, short wave to someone higher up the beach, reached back for a battered suitcase, and disappeared into the crowd. The next two were unfamiliar faces—obviously new teachers. They appeared to be fresh from the Lower 48 and wore frozen smiles as their eyes darted over the silent crowd, hoping to catch a sign of acknowledgment from someone.

Finally, a local man dressed in a light-tan bush jacket, green work pants and high rubber boots stepped forward, to awkwardly introduce himself and inquire if they were, indeed, teachers. Receiving a positive reply, he called out to two young boys and commandeered them into showing the teachers to their new quarters. Shyly, the boys took some of the waiting luggage and started on a side boardwalk, leading away from the beach to some back-houses. The two new teachers sought the boys' names and, bending over to catch the pronunciation of their last names, disappeared around a corner.

Cal turned back to the plane as more people unloaded. *I wonder how long those two will last,* he thought; every year some would just up and leave for good.

"Hey, Cal, you see that first one to get off? Ho, what a looker!" Cal's attention was diverted by a young fisherman standing beside him, who gave him a sharp swat on the shoulder.

"Yeah, alright, take it easy," Cal growled.

"I wonder what she teaches... maybe photography in the darkroom." The small group chuckled and jostled each other.

"Nah, she's the new basketball coach. Didn't you catch those long legs under that skirt?" Laughter again—this time from Lawrence. "I wish she'd come down off the Goose again!"

This time Cal had to laugh, too. It was rather funny when her skirt got caught on the steep stairs, pulling the hem well up her thighs. *She was kind of good-looking, too,* Cal decided, even though she was a little red in the face by the time she got unhooked.

That little incident gave the older men standing higher up the beach a good chuckle, their tanned, weathered faces wrinkling up to their ears. One young, Filipino cannery worker even whistled.

God! A skirt out here! Cal mused. Well, she'd learn. But it'd take her a year to live that one down—if even by then.

The last passengers to disembark were a couple dressed in old hiking boots, army fatigue pants, down vests and carrying small, well-worn backpacks. Behind them, a beautiful silver-black and white Siberian husky jumped from the plane. With little ado, the couple began collecting their various boxes and duffel bags, and stacked them on the beach. The local man in the tan bush jacket again stepped forward to greet the newcomers, and pointed out the teacher housing. The husband—a tall, dark-haired man with a large, drooping mustache—thanked the man then started up a conversation with the pilot, obviously discussing the flight over. His wife, also tall, with long, brown hair tied in a braid down her back, busied herself with their dog, Princess—Cal caught the name. As he took this all in, Cal felt there was something different about this couple. They seemed to have been around awhile. They were at ease in this presumably new environment. His curiosity aroused, Cal watched as the man and his wife started walking in the direction they were shown, backpacks slung over the shoulder, delighting in the antics of Princess, who was clearly glad to get off the plane. They didn't even take all their belongings—just left them on the beach for later—unlike the other new teachers, who tried to haul everything on the first trip.

With the main show over, the crowd slowly broke up, each person or group going back to their previous tasks.

Cal and the girls started drifting back toward the cannery,

pausing in front of the Sally Ann. This was a sort of hangout for the older kids in Biorka: a little snack shop with a jukebox and booths, serving hamburgers, fries and sodas. It was one of old Dan Zacharof's brainstorms about twelve years ago—just one of his many ideas. "Something to keep the kids out of mischief," he had always said. And a way to line his pockets, too, had said the Larsens. Nearly everything Dan started the Larsens criticized. The argument was still going on, although most of the younger Zacharofs and Larsens tried to stay out of the feud.

Just before the engines of the Goose barked to life and drowned all other sounds, Cal pivoted abruptly toward the cannery and shuffled off. "I gotta go."

"Yeah, me too," Lawrence added, as he followed Cal.

"See ya," several girls' voices chimed in, as they turned in the opposite direction.

Mail and passengers loaded, the plane again revved its engines to a high pitch, and the revived, bulky beast rolled ponderously toward the lapping waves. With a burst of fire and wind, the plane finally assumed new grace, as it sped off over the water and lifted delicately into the air, to seek its next stop, twenty minutes away at Unalga Airport: the nearest place where normal-wheeled RAA aircraft could land. The plane would make two more trips that day and three the next. It had to take advantage of the clear weather to bring in the remaining teachers, returning students, mail, and other miscellanies necessary to live in this small Alaskan town—perched like a small limpet shell on a wave-lashed boulder, struggling to keep its grip on a tiny piece of earth which provided grudging sustenance.

Before turning away from the group, Cal caught Catherine's glance and held it for a moment. With a slight nod, he turned back up the boardwalk with an unhurried gait.

Watching the two boys move on their way, Catherine felt a warmth rising in her, flushing her cheeks and warding off the chill of the wind. She knew she would probably see Cal later that day, or maybe tomorrow—that's what he had said... Well, he hadn't actually said it, but it was what he had meant, with the look and nod. That was Cal's way, and it was the way of most Biorka boys and men. *They don't talk much,* Catherine mused, *but you can pick up what they mean.* After all, they had grown up and spent most of their lives together, so they knew each other pretty well. The girls of Biorka had mostly grown up together, too, but somehow they still felt the need to talk more.

"I gotta go," Alice abruptly stated. A general chorus of agreement sounded, as other girls spoke up and headed off.

The older girls walked on past the post office, where Ruth turned and waved Alice and Catherine off. The other two girls continued, lost in private thoughts.

At her house, Alice turned to Catherine. "You going to see him tonight?"

"Maybe," she acted uninterested in the possibility, but not really. "I might see him at the Sally Ann, if I go down tonight."

"Well, watch it, kid," Alice offered, somberly. "He reminds me of my father." With that, she ducked inside the porch of her house and disappeared.

Catherine stood rooted to the ground for a few seconds, surprised and confused at Alice's words. *What the hell did she mean by that?* Catherine wondered.

Damn, it makes me mad when she does things like that! Alice acts so weird sometimes, she fumed, as she turned away, toward her home. *I know she's pretty mature for her age, but still…*

A sharp gust of wind struck Catherine's face and pulled her attention away from Alice. Looking out onto the bay, she watched as dancing fingers of a fresh breeze stirred the water's surface with a flourish, sending widening curves of wavelets driving toward the shore. The sharp smell of the salt air tickled her nose, and Catherine tossed her long, black hair in the wind, enjoying the tingling sensation the experience gave her. How she loved that feeling of aliveness and freedom!

Giving herself to the child which still lay hidden within, Catherine ran the remaining short distance to her house, as fast as she could.

But a week later, just to the southeast of Biorka, in a village nestled along the shore, the freshening wind was bringing a tempest of another kind…

3
Village

Paul

Paul was breathing heavily now that he was at last almost at the summit of his favorite mountain. Well, it wasn't truly a mountain, such as the snow-capped, volcanic cones farther inland, but he liked to think of it as a mountain.

He had always laid claim to it, for as many of his twelve years as he could remember. In the summer, it stood welcoming and green, its grasses rolling in the wind, like the waves of the bay below. In winter it looked grim, with the topmost rocks rearing up as ice-encrusted horns, above the more gentle slopes below.

Turning his thoughts back to the task at hand, Paul Surikov strained to wedge his way past the final two summit rocks, which the village children called the "Devil's Horns". Stepping up, he turned to his right, climbed monkey-style to the top of the higher rock and inched out flat on his belly, to the edge of the precipice.

Just as a tossed rock sends out ripples in a pond, Paul's eyes scanned down the steep drop to the green grass below. They followed its waving expanse along the slope, as it stretched in ever-widening vistas, until his eyes filled with the distant motion of the grass and sea against the dark, hulking mountains. Like a broken string of pearls, the few buildings of the tiny village of Ichinski nestled at the foot of Paul's hill, tightly hugging the curved shore of Nizki Bay, which was about thirty miles southeast of Biorka.

Ichinski was sited just to the east of a large bluff rising a hundred feet above the beach. From that vantage point, the whole of the bay could be seen, and it was for this reason that early Aleut settlers picked this place to establish their homes.

As migrating whales and other sea mammals rounded Cape Dora to the southwest, they were easy to spot. The dark, moving hordes of salmon were also clearly seen, as they came in from the sea to school in front of their designated spawning streams. Caribou could also be sighted on distant hillsides, as they migrated from one interior valley to another.

Yes, the site was well chosen and had been occupied continuously for at least five hundred years.

Paul lay on the rock, his gentle, oval face cupped in his hands, beaming with pride at the thought of his ancestors striking out in small boats of skin—called baidarkas—to pursue the whales in their spring migration to the north. Even in his grandparents' generation, a few had been taken, and his grandfather's story of how one harpooned beast had beached at Barren Point, a day's paddle to the southeast, and whose meat had to be brought back to Ichinski, never failed to make Paul proud.

What men! Aleut men! How he wished he could take his paddle out in such a boat and hunt today! But Grandfather died when Paul was eight, and since then it had become increasingly difficult to conjure up the reality of those vanished days. It wasn't just missing his grandfather; something else was gone. Paul could never quite put his finger on it, and the thought disturbed him at times like this.

Lost in his musings, Paul failed to see two small, distant figures emerge from the village and begin winding their way up the hill. As they approached, they waved their arms and shouted Paul's name, finally catching his eye as his gaze drifted downward, with the swoop of a bald eagle he had been watching. Lifting himself off the rock, he could see that they were his cousins Willie and Mary Andreanof, aged eight and fourteen, with whom he had played all his life.

They might know something about my dad coming back, Paul realized, and resigned himself to heeding their frantic summons.

He cast one more sweeping glance upon the village below: its small, onion-domed, Russian Orthodox church looking out of place amongst the plain, box-shaped houses and sheds; the lush green grass rolling in waves toward the shore, and swallowed up by the blue-green sea; the miles-long, rocky crescent beaches sweeping the sides of Nizki Bay. He gazed over at the mountains, rising bare-headed almost from the shore, and reaching back inland in folding wrinkles, until the snow-topped, volcanic cones of the interior peaks were reached. All of these were like old friends to Paul, since from this spot he could take them in at one glance and put them into their proper place and perspective.

The world never quite looked the same from down below, and he felt swallowed up by it. But here he was king, and it was all his, to have and admire. Reluctantly, he placed his hands on either side of the Horns, and swung out and down into the world below.

Willie and Mary did have some news to tell Paul, but it wasn't about his father. It was about the school; it was going to be closed this year! They knew nothing more than that—not how long or why—just that it was being closed.

Paul stood there awkwardly, at a loss for words, and looked at the grinning faces of his cousins. All three children stood stock still, relishing the joy of a shared miracle, then burst into a whopping chorus.

They looked ever so much like three apes dressed in rags, as they jumped and pounced and rolled their way down the grassy slope. Laughing and tumbling, they finally came to a flat spot, where the inertia of their bodies slowed, and the self-infecting lunacy was forced to retreat. Gasping for air, they lay on their backs and let the reality of the scudding clouds and nodding grass sink in.

A few moments of silence passed, then Paul asked: "Who said it was closed?"

"John Kristovich did," Mary blurted; "you know, Freddy's dad. He came over from Biorka just now. He said so."

Paul didn't answer, letting the names sink in. Why was Freddy's dad here before the others? "What's John doin' here? Where's my dad?" Paul still had his original interest in mind.

"Who cares about your dad?! Don't you care that school is closed? That means we won't have to sit in that stupid old building this year. It gives me the creeps!"

Mary's words started to register. Memories flooded Paul's

mind, and immediately he recoiled in disgust. Yes, they all had reason to dislike that building. It was where, just last spring, Charlie Benson stabbed little Julia Vernofski to death in their classroom.

He had stormed into the small room, waving a butcher knife and yelling at Julia that Chi Chi, her mother, wasn't going to get away with treating him like caribou dung, just because he sometimes drank too much. He was soused at the time, but still sober enough to convince everybody that he was serious.

All the kids had seen neighbors and relatives drunk and threatening before—that wasn't anything new; besides, the kids could easily escape and hide—but this was different. Charlie went straight for Julia, lunging right over the desks, and he didn't fall or stumble. Julia leaped for the hallway and everybody else flew for the windows, closets or under the desks. Charlie ended up stabbing her five times before she died. Then, he just turned and walked off home. Most of the kids and Miss Richards, the new B.I.A. teacher, were still in the classroom when he caught Julia, and they saw the entire struggle.

As soon as some adults were summoned and poor little Julia's body was taken home, Miss Richards set off and walked ten hours straight, around the bay and overland, to get to Biorka. And she never came back; never even sent for her belongings. A couple of state troopers flew in two days later from Sandpoint, and finally coaxed Charlie out of his house without having to shoot him.

Of course, Paul shared Mary's happiness of not having to

attend school in that building this year, but at the moment he was more concerned about his father. He had promised Paul a new pair of hip boots from this latest trip to Biorka; the ones he now had on were three sizes too big, full of patches and had the inner lining stringing down, where they were folded back to his knees. He was proud to have any hip boots at all—the mark of a fisherman—but he still wanted some new ones.

His dad had gone for supplies with Uncle James and Zeke Andreanof—Willie and Mary's dad. Dick Surikov usually made this supply run to Biorka every two or three weeks, with Zeke and James, depending on need and weather. If fishing was good in the summer, they went whenever they beach-seined enough salmon to sell to the cannery. They then bought groceries and other necessities at the company store.

Sometimes, though, they all got to drinking in the Idle Hour Bar, or partying at somebody's house, and wouldn't get back to Ichinski until a day or two later. By then, most of the fish money had been spent and the men would come back with ashen faces, defensive about their actions and carrying very few groceries. Paul always felt sick when the men silently beached the skiffs and somberly stepped ashore; he knew what had happened in town.

However, if the men came back the same day they left, everybody rushed to greet them. They would yell and wave to everyone, and Paul would know his dad had kept his promises. It would be a festive time, with lots to eat. True, they always brought back some beer and whiskey for a bit more drinking that night, but at least everyone was cheerful. Besides, when the drinking became excessive and quarrels broke out, the kids just retreated to their favorite hiding places and gorged on snacks all night.

Since Dick and the other men were already two days overdue, Paul had about resigned himself to no new boots and a week of tough living at home. He didn't mind cooking, washing dishes or taking care of his uncle, dad and grandma while they recovered; what Paul hated most was that his dad wouldn't take him out fishing or hunting for the meat they badly needed, since the grocery money had been spent. After a good trip to Biorka, his dad would always take him out and show him different tricks for finding game, but when the men blew their money, Dick would always go out hunting alone, with a vengeful air, as if seeking to re-establish his prowess and worth as a man of the village.

"Aleut men are hunters and fishermen," his dad would often say. "You gotta learn to be one, too. Any fool can go work in the cannery or sit at a desk to earn money, but only an Aleut man is smart enough and tough enough to live out here with his bare hands." It was something within the Aleut, his dad would add, that made them able to live here.

Paul guessed his dad must be right about being strong, because he had told Paul about fights he'd had with outsiders, while he was staying out at Anchorage. Dick said it was his Aleut cunning, born of practice in hunting, that always helped him win. Paul didn't quite see the connection of all this, and sometimes doubted if his dad could always beat everybody up, especially since he often came back from Biorka in rather sad shape for a winner.

But that was adult stuff and not Paul's concern. Right now,

Paul was worried about his boots—and that was all.

Somebody was yelling in the distance, and Paul turned to the bluff near town to see little Freddy Kristovich come running down it, shouting that the men were seen coming in their boats.

Paul's heart skipped and took one big bounce, into his throat and down again. How he hoped those shiny boots were on his dad's boat!

Everyone else had heard Freddy's thin cry, too, because other people of the village started appearing and moving toward the beach. The children were the most excited, with expectations of granted requests soaring, and they went to the water's edge to wait. Besides the two Andreanof children, John Kristovich's four youngsters were there, and three children from two other families.

The adults all stayed back at the top of the beach, or sat down on their doorsteps to see what would happen. A return from Biorka was old hat to them, but there was usually little else to do at the moment, so they turned to watch what the sea would bring them this time.

Paul's grandma, Nyda, was standing with the watchers. She was in her late sixties and looked as though she had paid dearly for each of those years, a slightly stooped walk making her more diminutive than she was. Her now weather-hardened, wrinkled, brown face had once been the envy of every girl living in Tanaik, the village of her birth, four hundred miles farther out on the Aleutian Islands; many a young man had vied for the chance to go to the far cliffs of the island with her, to collect murre and seagull eggs. The liveliness and wit of her youth now returned only when she was well plied with liquor.

Looking at Paul's thin frame, lightly clad despite the chilling wind, she could remember those times past when her son Dick used to wait for his father, and she for hers. To her, it seemed like the people of the islands had always been waiting for something from the sea, never knowing whether it would be animals to hunt, fish to net, news to make you think deeply, or foreigners to bring new ways and confuse your mind. *We all learn to wait, and Paul must learn, too,* she thought, as the two skiffs ground noisily onto the stony beach. She watched as Paul rushed up to the water's edge and waited expectantly with the other children.

Paul had trouble sleeping that night, after the men's arrival; not that noise or people talking was keeping him awake. Ichinski was always dead quiet at night, except for the frequent storms or those nights when people sang, played music or simply talked about past times or new events, sometimes loosened with a little alcohol. No, it was a feeling which kept him awake; an uneasiness about something.

It had started to gradually grow on Paul shortly after his father and the other men arrived. Contrary to what everyone expected, the men hadn't been waylaid in the Idle Hour, although they did spend one evening swapping stories and a few drinks at Don and Clara Kristovich's house (John's younger brother, who had moved his family from Ichinski to Biorka, a few years ago). As far as Paul could figure out, they had bought the supplies they were supposed to—no new boots for Paul, though—and spent the rest of the time doing some "business", as Zeke had put it.

There wasn't the usual party that night, either; the children were all fed a good meal and sent to bed. Paul was excited about the frosted cake and ice cream the men brought. He'd had store ice cream many times before, but this time the kids had three gallons to gorge on, packed in ice from the cannery so that it wouldn't melt too much—and it was a feast!

As for the adults, they all went to John's house and talked. It was just the Kristovichs, Andreanofs, Millers and Paul's dad there; the Bernstens and Dirks didn't go. The Dirks were an old couple without kids, and they went back home.

The Bernstens were fairly new, having moved back from Kodiak to live closer to the wife's parents. The young couple married just four years ago and had a three-year-old daughter—a fat little thing everyone called JuJu. Not having older children, they stayed back to keep an eye on the sleepers.

This wasn't at all how it usually was. The children were always permitted to stay up late the night after a successful trip, and the parents never sat and just talked like this. Paul was sure something was up, but he couldn't figure out what. However, despite his concern, tired from his climb up the mountain, he eventually drifted off to sleep.

He dreamed of stomping around in a spawning stream, with shiny new hip boots; silver and pink salmon jumping every which way as he scooped them up with a big, sparkling gold dip-net.

The next morning, when he went into the kitchen for breakfast, his dad and James were already eating. Grandma was frying up some caribou strips and pancakes on the woodstove, mentioning something about Paul needing it for today's journey.

The crackling fire and smell of alder burning had always made the kitchen Paul's favorite place in the house. It was warm at least twice a day and, when Grandma was feeling good, she would often have small snacks for Paul to curl up with beside the big stove.

As Paul sat down at the table, his dad commented: "Come on down to the beach when you're done and help launch the skiff. We're goin' back to Biorka today, and you're comin' along." With that, he stood up and went outside.

Uncle James looked up from eating and, chewing his meat thoughtfully, stared at Paul for a moment, then went back to his plate. James's look puzzled Paul; it was as if his uncle were trying to tell him something. But, since James wasn't one to talk very much—particularly not to Paul—he quickly dropped his eyes to start on the pancakes and meat.

As he chewed, the full flavor of the fried caribou strips and sweetness of the syrupy pancakes became more interesting than the strange look James had given him.

The wind was gusting rather heavily that day, with sheets of rain coming down in squalls every few minutes. Nizki Bay was full of marching whitecaps, and Paul wondered why they had to make the run to Biorka on this particular day, since the men had just been there the day before. As he made his way to the beach, Paul tripped on a piece of driftwood, which lay half-buried in the rock and sand.

"Come on, I want t'get back early this afternoon," his dad chided. "Don't be so clumsy and get movin'."

The skiff was at the top of the beach, and they had to pull it to the water. James leaned into the bowline thrown over his shoulder, while on each side Paul and his father half-carried, half-dragged the boat. It was a task Paul never liked because, being small, he always nearly got run over by the boat. The skiff wasn't long—only about seventeen feet—but it was heavy. Once, Paul got his foot caught between the boat and a large rock, and it scraped rather badly. But, since the surf was high and the moment of launching was at hand, he had to swallow his tears and climb aboard, or be left behind. The water was like that today, and Paul fervently hoped he wouldn't stumble again.

With the boat poised for the final push, Dick and James brought down the outboard motor and an extra gas can, while Paul steadied the surging skiff. They fastened the motor tightly to the stern, threw the gas can in and, after an especially large series of waves, shoved the skiff out with the ebbing water. Paul only banged his left shin leaping aboard, and considered himself lucky.

As the motor caught and Dick headed the boat into the waves, Paul crawled back under the small canvas cover in the bow and settled down. The small boat was soon lost amidst the heaving swells and intermittent sheets of rain.

As the skiff pitched sharply from one steep sea to another, Paul's curiosity about what could draw the men out to make a trip on a day like this increased.

Yesterday and today have been very different, that's for sure, Paul thought. *What could be at Biorka?*

As the boat lurched suddenly, and a shower of spray flew over the shelter, Paul's head banged against a rib of the boat, and he figured he had better pay more attention to staying in one piece than wondering about grown-up business.

4
Town

Cal

The weather in Biorka on this day was quite a change from the previous ones of warmth and stillness. The wind blew with good strength, frequently pushing off-balance the bundled shapes of children hurrying to school on the boardwalks, for a step or two. Stinging sheets of rain accompanied the wind, adding to the difficulty of walking.

Inside the school building, it was warm and brightly lit, yet rather quiet. The stillness was broken only by the wind gusting against the building, or the teachers talking in the hallway. Today was the first day of school in Biorka, and the building was coming to life after its summer rest, as teachers made last-minute preparations and children scurried into the entrance corridor, to escape the weather. Like some kind of fortress refuge, the building stood, its metal roofing occasionally banging, windows rattling with the wind, and leaks from the ceiling appearing mysteriously. Yet it was always warm, bright and windless—in stark contrast to outside.

As Cal walked past the Sally Ann and turned away from the beach on a side boardwalk, he was glad to have the wind at his back. He shivered a little and considered buttoning up his heavy jean jacket, but now that the school building was in sight and he saw a group of older students outside the corridor, he rejected the idea. Hunching over a little more, as a sheet of rain came sweeping by, he shoved his hands deeper into his pockets and sauntered over toward the group.

"Hi, Cal," several voices offered. Cal nodded and mumbled a greeting.

After a brief silence, one boy spoke up: "Hey, where'd you go after you left Al Olsen's last night?"

Cal glanced up at the lanky figure. It was Mark Odegaard, and he had a sly grin on his sun-browned, boyish face. His straight, black hair lofted down to the shoulders of his blue down jacket; a Greek fisherman's cap was perched on the back of his head.

Cal didn't know anyone else had been out that late. "Nowhere," Cal countered.

"Aw, come on, I saw you. I was just leaving Popeye's," Mark insisted.

Cal knew he was caught; no sense bluffing. "Just having some fun with the girls from the bunkhouse." He was referring to the dormitory the cannery provided for imported seasonal workers. He had been there with two girls from Fairbanks, drinking and horsing around.

"Where were you going? Over to Lisa's?" Cal accused.

At this, the other boys who were listening broke up laughing. Lisa was a local gal, divorced and rather free with her affection. Mark and Cal looked at each other and laughed, too.

A bell rang and the waiting students began to push inside.

"Nice way to start the year, eh?" Mark suggested with a grin, referring to his and Cal's previous night's escapade. On this note, the boys all strode into the school, laughing and shoving each other about.

That morning went rather uneventfully for Cal. The new principal strutted about during an assembly in the gym, saying something about how this year they were going to crack down on discipline, that the students were here to learn and not to play around, and that he would get to know everybody personally. Cal sat up on the top row of the bleachers with some of his friends, and they spent the time making cracks about the principal's antics.

Cal's classes didn't impress him much, either: first, Campbell for business education and study hall, then senior English, taught by the new mustached teacher he had seen with the dog at the beach, when the Goose unloaded: his name was Jim Irving.

More importantly, Irving was also the new basketball coach. Cal had wondered who would handle that job, and he spent the class time trying to size up the man.

At last, the lunch bell finally rang, and the students exploded into the hallway. Cal walked leisurely along with Lawrence, glancing into the elementary classrooms, noticing their brightly colored bulletin boards and small desks. A twinge of memory passed over Cal as, once again, for a few fleeting seconds, he remembered how it felt to be small again, in the protective womb of such an environment.

5
Town

Paul

At that same moment, Dick Surikov's skiff ground over the pebbles, up onto the beach in front of the Biorka health clinic. Paul had been out from under the bow cover as soon as the town was sighted, and was glad to get out of the tossing boat.

Along with James, he leaped onto the beach and, grasping the side of the boat, held it against the drag of the receding wave. With the next wave swirling about their boots, James and Paul managed to guide the skiff farther up the beach, out of immediate danger.

Paul glanced around him. It had been two months since he had been to Biorka, and the memory of the last trip rushed in and made his heart race with expectation. How could he forget the pop and candy, that huge dinner with the Kristovich's and seeing those shiny new boots in the store? Paul didn't know why they had made this trip, but his mouth fairly watered with the prospect of a repeat performance. Eagerly, he added his strength to hauling the skiff above the high tideline.

Throwing the bow tarp back over the spare gas can, Dick grunted, "Let's go," and the three started down the boardwalk.

Before they reached the Sally Ann, the men turned off onto a side boardwalk, leading by the school. Following closely behind, Paul began to wonder what was up. He still had visions of wallowing in empty pop cans and candy bar wrappers, but began to think he might have to postpone that ecstasy, since they were apparently going visiting first.

Opposite the school building, the men suddenly stepped off of the boardwalk, crossed the rutted, muddy roadway and approached the entrance. Now a sickening feeling of confusion and fear raced through Paul. What was happening? *Why are they going in there?* Paul desperately struggled with his thoughts. Besides the cannery, the school building was the biggest thing Paul had ever seen and, to him, it loomed as a voluminous cave, in which people were swallowed up.

He had stood outside it several times before, in summers past, peering cautiously into its dark interior. It didn't help to be told it was a school, since "school" was what they had in Ichinski: a small, warm place just big enough for the teacher, Paul and eleven other children he had grown up with. It was incomprehensible to Paul how this could also be a school.

With trepidation, Paul followed the men inside, through the double doors. Just as he stepped out onto the red carpeting, the significance of what was happening thundered down upon him.

Greg Parkhurst, the principal, noticed the men—dressed in well-worn, gray coveralls and rubber boots—as they entered the corridor. Automatically, his body stiffened slightly and his face tightened perceptibly, at the corners of his mouth. He waited until the men had entered his office and stood silently in front of the desk for several seconds, before he shuffled some papers together and looked up, smiling.

"Good afternoon, gentlemen. What can I do for you?"

Stammering at first, Paul's father spoke up: "I-I-I got this boy here. He… the school at Ichinski got closed this year. My boy needs to go to school. Paul—" he shoved the boy forward, "get up here."

Paul emerged from behind the men, and stood as though naked before this square-built man, sitting and looking at him with a forced smile. The man, the huge steel desk, the stacks of papers, the typewriter, the copy machine, the huge picture windows… it was all too much for him, especially when he was thrust up so close. Paul dropped his eyes and stared at the patches on his hip boots.

After a pause, Parkhurst broke in with a spirited, official tone: "Yes, we have a letter from the B.I.A. office in Anchorage about the closure, and we are assuming stewardship of their former responsibility." He emphasized the words "have" and "assuming". Parkhurst had a habit of stressing words as he spoke, having always appreciated the effect his former superior officers in the Army achieved when dealing with subordinates.

Looking at the blank stares which greeted his pronouncement, Parkhurst added: "We'd be glad to have your son in school."

Dick Surikov was visibly relieved. He had been expecting some difficulty—there always was with people who worked in offices, especially when they were white men—but it looked like this was going to be pretty easy. *Now, ask about a place for Paul to stay,* he told himself, *then we can get out of here.*

"He needs a place to stay. Somebody's got to look after him. He's a good boy… He…"

"Yes, yes, I'm sure we can manage to find a suitable boarding home," Parkhurst broke in, finally showing some warmth on the subject. "Don't worry about the boy; he'll do fine," he added, with a broad smile.

"Okay," Dick replied with obvious enthusiasm, and reached out to pump Parkhurst's hand.

He turned to Paul, still standing ashen-faced and trembling, as he struggled to keep up with the flow of conversation. "Paul," Dick began, squaring the boy to face him, "now, you study hard here and don't cause no trouble with the people you stay with. You be a good boy, and mind your manners like I taught you."

With that load off his shoulders, Dick straightened up, beamed at Parkhurst and, with an awkward nodding half-bow, he turned and fled the office and building.

Uncle James, who had been silently watching the entire affair, now looked down at the boy. "See ya, Paul." He shifted his look up to the smiling Parkhurst, fixed him with a penetrating gaze, and turned out of the office.

Relieved to have the men out of his office, Parkhurst set his eyes on the small, quaking figure before him. *My God, that's all I need today. As if I don't already have my hands full!*

Parkhurst surveyed his new charge, starting from Paul's patched hip boots, up past the tattered, green coat, to the unruly, bowl-cut thatch of straight, black hair peeking out from underneath an orange cap. Sucking in his breath, he began: "Well, now, young man, what grade were you in at Ichinski?"

Silence.

"Come, now, don't be bashful. I won't bite you." A poor choice of jest.

More silence.

"Okay, let me get that letter from Anchorage, and we'll see what they had down." Parkhurst sorted through a stack of papers on his desk. "Ah, it says you're starting the seventh grade. Good. We'll get you a class schedule figured out later. Right now, I want you to go into Mrs. Irving's class. She's teaching social studies."

After writing a note to himself about locating a boarding home for Paul, he straightened up from his desk and walked around to the boy. With a hand lying heavily on his shoulder, he steered Paul out of the office and down the hallway; "Let's go, champ!"

The rest of Paul's day was similarly disastrous. He had no idea of where he was, what he was doing, or what he was supposed to be doing.

But at least the teachers were kind and smiled at him. They gave him books to look at and some placement tests to work on, though he was so confused by the multitude of different faces, and all the activity going on, that he found it difficult to concentrate long enough to do even a little of the task he was asked to do.

And the building was no better. When the hallways were

empty, the size was intimidating, but when the bells rang and classes changed, the jostling of students' bodies was overwhelming. It seemed to be a labyrinthine trap, with no escape.

The other students were confusing to him, as well. Most of them merely ignored his presence. Others made remarks he couldn't hear clearly, but he was sure he didn't like, because of the way other nearby students snickered. A couple of kids about his age talked with him, but they were often the butts of jokes themselves. The worst thing was that Paul couldn't distinguish which kids would react in which way to him.

By the end of the day, he had learned one important thing at school: stay quiet and keep to yourself. It was lonely that way, but safe. When the last bell rang and school was out for the day, Paul glued himself to a niche in the hallway, until the rush was past and it was fairly quiet. He then walked slowly down the carpeted hall, toward the front entrance.

As he passed by the gym doors, he paused for a moment, trying to catch a few lingering fragrances of the hot lunch he'd had in there, after a teacher discovered he hadn't eaten since early morning. How strange that had been! There was a funny rectangular plate, all divided up into little squares, with food in each one, and the whole thing wrapped up in shiny foil. Some of the food was rather strange, but the potatoes, gravy and peas he had eaten before. And, boy, was it hot! On the first bite he burnt himself. But that was alright, Paul decided, because the food was really good. His mouth watered at the thought of that tray of food—and the extra one he ate, too*! If I can get this every day,* he paused to think, *maybe this kind of* *school won't be too bad. At least it's something to look forward to.*

Principal Parkhurst noticed Paul standing out in the hallway and called him over, to tell him to wait about fifteen minutes in the corridor. Paul obeyed, wondering what this was about now. He didn't think he had done anything bad yet, though he did giggle in class once or twice.

After a while, Parkhurst emerged from his office, putting on his cap and plaid mackinaw coat. "Let's go, Paul."

They started walking up the road in front of the school, which led to the beach. There, they turned onto the beach boardwalk. After passing a few buildings, they turned again, to walk up the steps to a door that had a large, red cross painted on it. Above the door, it read: *"Health Clinic."* Parkhurst pulled twice on a cord, which rang a bell inside.

Shortly, a woman's voice called for them to come in, and they stepped inside.

Margaret Roman had been the nurse in Biorka for a little over a year now. She had previously been assigned to Aniok, on the Kuskokwim River delta of western Alaska, so she was no newcomer to rural Alaskan conditions. She was a robust woman of fair figure, twenty-eight years old and considered good-looking by her frequent suitors. Her slightly freckled face, with lightly tanned cheeks, and straw-colored hair pulled back in a ponytail, gave her a fresh, wholesome look that one wishes every nurse had. She never wore a uniform—she considered the suggestion absurd—but preferred well-worn blue jeans, white tennis shoes and a tucked-in checkered shirt, with long sleeves rolled up. Dressed in this manner, Margaret stepped up to greet her visitors.

"Hi, there. Come on in!" she effused, as she opened the door. "And this must be Paul!" She looked from Paul to Parkhurst and back, to beam at Paul. "How do you do, Paul? My name is Margaret." Then, she offered with a smile: "Hello, Greg."

Parkhurst was always slightly overwhelmed by the young nurse's vitality, and this time was no exception. He tried to regain the initiative. "Hello, Margaret. Yes, this is the boy. Are you sure you can manage him for a few days?" he asked, with excessive concern. "I know you don't have much room here, but it will sure help us out until we can find him a permanent home."

"No problem at all," Margaret assured him. Turning to Paul, she smiled: "How old are you?"

Paul looked up at the warm face, and into the nurse's sincere eyes. "Twelve," he blurted out involuntarily, his fear melting rapidly.

"Do you have any brothers or sisters?" she was still beaming at him.

"I got a sister, but I don't know where she is. I mean," Paul was getting uncomfortable, and he stiffened, "she's out Anchorage, or someplace like that. Anyway, that's what Uncle James told me." His palms began to sweat.

Sensitively, and with the same warm smile, Margaret eased Paul out of his difficulty. "Well, we have lots of time to talk about your family later. Right now, let's get you settled. Where are your things?" She peered behind the boy and onto the porch, then at Parkhurst. Paul flushed again and shifted his weight. His head dropped.

"He, ah, came as he is," Parkhurst fumbled, then gained control. "His father is probably going to send his things over soon, but until then you might call the chapel to check on their donation supply, in case he needs additional apparel," Parkhurst added, with a wink.

With that, he turned to go. "Well, I've got business to attend to, so I'll leave you two to get acquainted."

Turning to Paul, he added: "Paul, I'll see you in school tomorrow." Then, in mock seriousness, he wagged a finger; "And don't be late!" Paul only stared at him.

Parkhurst looked up to the nurse with a benevolent smile and another wink. "Just give me a call if you need me, honey." Then, he was gone.

Staring after the closed door, Margaret felt a slight flush of anger burn her face. *Where did they ever dig him up?* she asked herself and shuddered slightly in repulsion.

Taking a deep breath, she turned to face her new charge.

In the middle of the room stood Paul, silent and waiting, his eyes eagerly searching the nurse's face, trying to read her intentions, her thoughts—seeking desperately to know what was waiting for him in the next few hours, minutes or even seconds. The wind outside gusted, and the draft down the stovepipe made the flame in the oil heater flare up and gurgle for a few brief seconds, before settling down to its former steady murmur.

"How about taking your coat and cap off?" Margaret encouraged.

Paul slowly pulled off the brilliant-orange, billed cap. Looking for a place to lay it down, he was aided by the nurse's outstretched hand. Encouraged, he more rapidly unbuttoned his dirty, torn coat and handed it to her. Looking quickly about, as she set his things in a corner, Paul noticed how clean and neat everything was, and he began to feel self-conscious about his clothes.

"Say," Margaret began, "I'll bet you'd like a nice, hot bath right now, to warm you up on such a cold evening, wouldn't you?"

Paul couldn't see that the weather was particularly cold, but as he followed the nurse to where the deep, ancient, claw-footed tub stood, the thought of all that hot water was inviting, he had to admit.

"And afterward, we'll have some hot cocoa and a snack."

That did it. Paul nodded and smiled slightly at her as he undressed. "Big tub," Paul quietly observed, as he kicked off his hip boots.

"Yes, it is. It's a good place to stretch out and relax," Margaret agreed, as she tried not to stare at the sores on Paul's feet, which had resulted from bare feet chafing on hard rubber. The last of his ragged clothing confirmed her expectations of a need for disinfectant.

"Just a minute, Paul," she cautioned before he stepped into the tub. "If you want to get really clean, we've got to use some of this first," she added, as she reached into the cabinet; "there's a little problem we need to take care of." She smiled confidently. Paul knew what this was all about; Grandma had treated him for scabies many times before, and he nodded to the nurse.

It was now almost ten o'clock—nearly an hour since he was put to bed on the couch in the nurse's living quarters. Paul had been lying there thinking about the day: the bath, the food, school, the nurse and Parkhurst, the trip over, his dad... It was all a jumble of images, which continually twisted and rolled over each other in his mind, never settling down so that he could order them into a meaningful sequence. So much had happened today—more than at any other time in his life.

What terrified him more was that he didn't know what would happen tomorrow, or the day after, or the next, or the next. When would his dad take him back to Ichinski? That place and all the memories it held seemed abruptly to be ages and millions of miles distant, as if in an ancient dream. *It shouldn't be that way,* Paul thought, as anger and tears welled up; *this should be the dream and Ichinski should be real!*

Finally, Paul could hold it no longer. Tears coursed down his freshly cleaned cheeks and fell onto the white sheets tucked under his chin. A soft whimpering rose in his chest and throat, sounding ever so much like a small puppy calling out in utter distress, while his mother is out hungrily feeding at her dish. He cried and tears flowed. And he gave himself, mind and body, to the anger, sadness and frustration of his situation. Why did his dad do this? What would happen to him now?

Slowly, the loneliness of his predicament overwhelmed all thoughts, and Paul withdrew into the shell of his body, his mind sinking slowly within, dropping deeper as exhaustion and sleep calmed him. The last thing Paul remembered, before going to sleep that night, was the seemingly distant rattle of a doorknob and click of a door, as it slowly set against its frame and the mechanism found its seat.

6
Questions

Catherine

The wall clock's minute hand was slowly inching toward the top of the clock face, in short, little jumps; once at the top, its function would be complete; then, it would be three o'clock and time to go home!

Catherine looked back from the clock to her desk. Staring up at her was an outline of dates, places and persons relevant to the earliest European colonial settlements in North America. She had decorated the margins of the papers with flowers, funny faces and names, and now she put her chin in her hand and slumped down to doodle with her pencil some more, as the teacher droned on in the background.

It was almost the end of September now—four weeks since school had begun; just long enough for the freedom of summer to become a fading memory. Not that this summer had been so great; she had spent most of it working steadily on the pack line in the cannery, because of the good fishing season. She told herself she enjoyed having the money, because she could buy a few extra clothes she wanted but, in reality, she saved most of her earnings.

For several months now, she'd had this nagging feeling

she would need these saved wages sometime soon, and she had worked hard to make money. Maybe that was the problem: work this summer hadn't been just for fun money, as in the past, but serious business. It made her feel, well, different somehow.

Perhaps it was that statement by Campbell, on the last day of economics class last year, about spending their earnings on frivolous things, and what they would do next year if the salmon run was poor and they had spent all their money. Most of his impassioned, five-minute speech was lost on Catherine, and all the other students as well, but the words "What will you do next year?" somehow stuck in her mind all summer, bringing on a quiet, grumpy mood that neither she nor her friends could understand.

If Catherine's summer hadn't been outstanding, neither was her senior year at school so far. Her English and history classes were boring, in her view. The Irvings were very sincere about what they were doing—that she had to admit—but, well... Who cares about transitional sentences and who got to America first? It just didn't touch her; didn't mean anything to her and her life in Biorka. It was the same with physical science. *Who cares where rocks came from, or how long the Earth will last before it burns up in the sun? What does that have to do with the price of Coke in the Sally Ann?*

Now, photography class was different! She wasn't doing much but fooling around with a camera, and the darkroom stuff was kind of like magic. She was making something happen—something she did all by herself.

The photography teacher was also the librarian, so

Catherine had Miss James (of hooked-skirt fame) for two periods. Catherine also liked her job as a library aide, because it gave her the chance to give order to and direct her personal life a little during school, and she could get out, walk around and talk to people. It was sort of like working behind the scenes, seeing how things happened and making them work, instead of always being on the receiving end. She hated just sitting at a desk and having this person, a teacher, trying to fill her mind with a burden of facts.

An intruding voice brought her back to the present: Mrs. Irving was finishing up a point in Alaska history class. "I want you to think about this over the weekend and come back prepared to discuss it on Monday. It is important."

Mrs. Irving looked at the class. No one was paying attention. A couple of students looked up at the clock—two minutes to three—then back to their desks. Someone groaned.

"I want you to be able to tell me what makes you think you are an Aleut." Heads went up. "Or, maybe you should consider yourselves more European; most of you have Russian or Scandinavian names. Why do you think you're Aleut?" She paused and reviewed the blank faces staring at her. "Think about it. I want some answers Monday." With that, she noisily flopped a book down on her desk and the bell rang.

Like everyone else, Catherine sat there for a moment. Then, the significance of the bell penetrated the stun of Mrs. Irving's words, and the class leaped for the door.

Catherine was on the window side of the room, so she was one of the last to leave the room. She glanced back at the teacher, now roughly shuffling books and papers, recklessly clearing off her desk and nearby shelves. She's angry, Catherine realized. *Why? What did we do?*

"Cath, let's go," a voice called from the hallway.

Catherine walked down the boardwalk with Alice and Ruth for a while, stopping along the way to gossip with friends. The sea was quite calm, but a succession of heavy swells kept up a continuous roar in the background. The talk was mostly about school and boys.

Soon the other girls left her. She was ready to turn the corner to her house when Cal appeared, walking toward her.

Cal had hurried on home after school, to change into working clothes, since his dad had sent word that there was a load of freight they had to move from the dock to home. He had just gotten started toward the dock when he spied Catherine. Setting his pace a little slower, he continued walking. "Hi, Cath," he greeted.

"Hi, Cal." She smiled and slowed a little, expectantly. They met and stopped. "Where you off to?"

"Oh, gotta go to the warehouse. We got some stuff in on the barge today, and my dad wants it off the dock. Got to get it home before someone swipes it," he added.

"Is there a lot?" Catherine asked, trying to keep the conversation going.

"Nah, not too much; it'll be done by seven."

Cal hesitated, pushed at some rocks with his boot. "Uh, Cath, you wanna go to the dance tomorrow night?" Cal felt excessively warm, all of a sudden.

Catherine looked straight into Cal's eyes as he said his piece. She knew she was making it tough on him, but why did he always have to be so bashful about asking, she wondered. They'd gone out together, off and on, for three years—known each other all their lives—yet it was still like the first time he had ever asked her!

"Sure, Cal, I'd like to," she finally smiled. "I hope a lot of kids show up; that'll make it good for the first dance this year." She added: "Why don't you ask Lawrence and Mark to be sure to come? Maybe they could talk it up with some of the other guys."

"Yeah, maybe so. I might see them down at the dock. I guess their families got some stuff in, too." He paused in relief.

"Well, I better get goin', or my old man'll beat me," he grinned. Cal got along great with his dad, like pals, and the thought of him beating Cal just for being a few minutes late was too ridiculous to picture. Catherine had to laugh, too. The sharing of this small joke warmed both of them, and they could feel the momentary bond of affection grow between them. They felt more at ease with each other and, after a few exchanged words, they passed by each other, turning to give a last smile and goodbye.

Saturday night, Catherine was at the school early, to help set up the stereo in the gym and get the snack bar stocked and ready. She was one of three girls who sort of managed the dances.

She dressed casually in jeans, but had taken care to make sure her appearance was a little extra special tonight. When Cal showed up at the dance, he hung around the corridor with some other guys, while she and a couple of other girls went into the restroom to check their appearance.

Catherine had especially beautiful hair: it was shiny jet-black, thick and wavy, and cascaded down to the middle of her back. Its dark color sat well against her softly rounded face, with a tinge of tan coloring highlighting her cheekbones. She stood five and a half feet tall and filled her mature figure well—not exactly overweight, but "firmly", as she liked to put it.

Tonight, she had put on a new, flowered top, with tastefully contrasting ruffles at the bottom hem and along the elbow-length sleeves. The neckline wasn't too high or too low, but just right, a little lower than Cal might have expected. *Might make him loosen up a little tonight,* she thought, when she selected it. The other girls were ready to go, and chatted gaily as they swung out the restroom door.

Cal had been shooting the bull with some guys when the girls came bouncing out. They were laughing and, to all appearances, oblivious to the existence of the boys in the corridor. Cal's eyes fastened on Catherine, as she came floating down the hall between the two other girls.

God, she looks sharp! Cal marveled, as they advanced. His eyes rapidly took in the shape of her figure, outlined well in form-fitting jeans, the flounce of the top flaring at the waist, and the neckline scooping suggestively at her well-formed bustline. A tingling sensation spread slowly from Cal's groin as his heart raced and skip.

"Hi, Cal," Catherine called cheerily, as the other girls greeted the boys.

"Hi, Cath," Cal replied, and he shuffled forward to meet her. He opened a space between his side and elbow, to allow her to slide her hand through and take his arm, as they walked into the dark, strobe-lit gym.

Despite a slow start, the dance didn't go too badly after all. Few kids showed until about 8:30 p.m., and it started picking up then. The time was spent talking, buying stuff at the snack bar and a little dancing. It was quite dark on the dancefloor most of the time, and the music was loud, so it made couples feel alone out there. As a result, Catherine and Cal enjoyed dancing the occasional slow dances, their bodies pressed closely together.

There was also some making out on the gym mats stacked behind the bleachers, where it was very dark. After the warmth of summer passed, there weren't too many spots around town where a boy and girl could get together very easily, since the rain and wind made it rather miserable to use any of the favorite haunts: under the docks or between some old cannery buildings. Of course, they could go to some friend's house whose parents were away, or somebody's fishing boat, but that took more scheming. Therefore, the dances were always popular places for necking. Safe, too, since the supervising teachers weren't too concerned, as long as the kids kept things within bounds.

Catherine and Cal sat on the mats and necked a little, but

most of the time they danced or wandered from group to group, chatting with friends.

On the way home that night, Catherine and Cal dawdled along the boardwalk, enjoying the still air, the bright moon partially veiled through scattered clouds, and the gentle rushing sound of the near-calm sea breaking on the graveled beach. They walked silently for the most part, now and then remembering something about the dance and sharing a laugh.

This is so nice, Catherine mused, as she glanced around then up at Cal. *Why can't he be loose like this all the time? When he's like this I feel like I can tell what he's thinking, and how he truly feels. But when he gets around other boys—or, worse, some fishermen just out of school—he acts completely different, as though he's an actor in a movie or on TV, trying to be something he's expected to be.*

Catherine tried to follow her thoughts further, but the conclusion escaped her. She knew she liked—yes, she could even say loved—him, when he was this private person. But, around others it was different, and this greatly confused her. *Which one is he, really?* she asked herself.

Shortly, they passed the Idle Hour, and it was rather lively inside. Three men on their way to the bar, reeling and laughing, passed them. Recognizing Cal, they called out: "Hey, Cal! What'cha got there?" Finally recognizing it was Catherine, they continued: "Hey, ol' man, you coming on down to Dan's place later?"

Catherine felt Cal—*her* Cal—slip away and the other Cal appear. "Alright, George? Okay, maybe I can make it," he grinned, and patted the nearest man soundly on the back.

"Good party goin' on. Don'cha miss it!"

"Okay, okay." Cal gave them a good-hearted shove to help them on their way.

Smiling as he turned back to her, Catherine saw that they had lost the special essence of the night, and she quietly announced: "I'd better get home."

Cal's grin fell as he picked up the coolness of her voice. "Yeah, I guess it's late."

Together, they walked silently to her house. He paused at the porch steps, hoping she would stop, but she took a couple of steps up the stairs.

Catherine sensed Cal's hesitancy, and even dared to hope that maybe he too wanted to remove the awkwardness and return the mood they had lost, but he said nothing. Digging his hands deeper in his pockets, he looked up, eyes pleading. Yet, he couldn't say anything; he wanted to, but somehow something wouldn't let him.

Catherine looked deeply, even sadly, at the imploring, turned-up face. *How can I help you?* her mind strained. *I don't know which one of you is you!* Vision blurred with tears, she turned and rapidly climbed the stairs, to disappear into the house.

Cal stood rooted for a minute, not fully comprehending the unspoken struggle between them, but sensing—hoping—that perhaps she had understood he was sorry. He felt weak and his throat tightened, as if to cry—something he had not done for a long time.

Then, the image of himself standing there like a little

puppy, almost whimpering, made him flush hot and glance around, to make sure no one had seen him. Gathering courage, he turned and angrily kicked a pop can along the boardwalk, making a resounding clatter in the darkness as it tumbled off, onto the gravel.

Damn, he thought, furiously, *what the hell do I care?!* Jeez, what if somebody had seen him mooning like that? He'd never be able to set foot on the deck of a fishing boat ever again.

Swelling with his regained pride and strength, Cal set off briskly and loudly toward Dan's place.

7
Hills

Paul

The young bald eagle, with wings outstretched, rose silently on the updraft from the mountain. Feeling the strength of the gust increasing, he met the force head-on, stretching his wing muscles even more, to take advantage of the full lifting force. Higher and higher he soared, circling in wide loops, the wind hissing loudly as it sped past his body and through his taut wing feathers. Suddenly, he broke the top of the draft and managed to lift out of the turbulence, catching the crest of the streaming sea of air, as it poured out from the craggy mountain top, over the lagoon below. The young eagle locked his wings and, never moving once for a half-minute, streaked out in a brown flash, across the deep valley containing the lagoon waters. Sensing the strength of his body and the power at his command, the young bird was urged by some deep-seated ancestral emotion burning within his being, to do yet something more—something to let the world know of his existence—and he cried out:

"Ri-ri-ri-ri! E-e-e-e-e!"

The starting chortling and following staccato whistling call was distinct and piercing, yet floated softly over the air to the far reaches of the valley.

In silence and awe, Paul continued following the course of the eagle, as it glided across the lagoon and entered the rocky fastness of the sharp peaks on the other side, before disappearing. He had been watching the eagle since it began its long climb up the draft, spellbound by the way it seemed to effortlessly lift to the top of the thermal. It was a scene he had seen many times before, over in the mountains and valleys near Ichinski, but he never tired of the spectacle. How he wished he could be an eagle: to fly, soar and be so free. What spectacular sights it must see! What a feeling it must be to tear through the air like that!

Paul's mind raced as he lay back on the springy tundra surface, hands locked behind his head, envisioning himself an eagle speeding through space, free and unencumbered. *Ah, yes! No school or any other distractions.* He dreamed blissfully for a few minutes.

But the eagle had now gone, and Paul's vision returned to earth, and the reality of memory and his existence.

The day had turned out to be one of those infrequent occurrences in the Aleutians when everything stands still: the wind, the sea, the clouds and even the sun seem to stop and linger, to enjoy the miracle; the resulting silence is surreal. Upon stepping outdoors, early in the morning, it appears that nothing anywhere is alive, so accustomed one is to the roar of the wind and surf. But, gradually, other sounds reach out tentatively—a songbird high on the hillside alder bushes; the cry of gulls fighting over cannery scraps; children laughing as they ride their bicycles over small jumps—and seem to float over the town and hillsides, in detachment from their source. On such a fine day, the entire population of Biorka was usually outside on their doorsteps, the beach or the hills; and Paul was one of the first to get outdoors that Sunday.

At the end of town was a lagoon, which extended back into the mountains approximately two miles. It was originally a part of the bay but, as ocean currents changed over the last several thousand years, a gravel bar built up from the south shore and extended out for a half-mile, to almost close off that part of the bay. That didn't happen, however, because three major stream systems drained into the lagoon, constantly washing away any bar segment which might otherwise develop. Thus, a wide channel of one hundred yards was kept open not only by the freshwater runoff, but additionally by the flooding and ebbing of the tides which continued to occupy the lagoon. In 1901, the village of Biorka was built on this grassy bar, which extends out from the shore of the large bay.

Paul walked along the lagoon road that morning, stopping occasionally to watch sandpipers working over a tide pool, or gulls pry out a tasty treat of mussel from its shell. The road ended with the lagoon, and Paul then followed a large stream at the lagoon's head, until it shortly spread out into several smaller streams.

There were still a few late humpies and some coho moving up the river to spawn, and Paul squatted beside the stream near a shallow bar eddy, to watch the female salmon dig nests with their tails. Hovering near and fighting off intruders, the male fish would swim over the open nest and release a cloud of sperm to fertilize the eggs, as soon as the female moved off. Once emptied of their burdens and the nest covered by the male's thrashing tail in the pebbles, they joined the other slow-moving, spawned-out fish, to swim in an endless procession against the current, until the rapid deterioration of their bodies was complete and their gills ceased to function. Everywhere Paul looked there were salmon in various stages of spawning, dying and decomposing.

He also frequently found signs of bears which had been feeding along the stream; here and there were carcasses of fish, stripped to the bone and left to accumulate on the bank. In the deeper grass of the small stream valley, paths were formed by the big brownies, as they scouted along the bank looking for unclaimed fishing spots. In places, the paths had been worn almost a foot deep from the years of travel.

Paul used these paths to travel on, because they were the best way to get around that unpredictable terrain. But, whenever the path led too close to or behind a dense thicket of alder bushes, he took a short side route. It was an automatic move he made, conditioned by the warnings of his dad and uncle, and by the true stories of bear attacks he had listened to as a young child.

The main stream had dwindled in size, and shortly Paul had to decide which way to go. Turning around to face downstream, he could see the buildings of the town at the far end of the lagoon. The only moving objects were a couple of pickups amongst the buildings. Higher than everything else stood the cannery complex and the school. Moved by a sudden feeling of aversion, he quickly decided to climb up the hillside to his left and aimed for a gap between two bordering hilltops. Setting off at a fast pace, he moved in a steady rhythm, born of experience with the terrain.

Halfway up a hillside spur, Paul stopped to lie back and rest. It was from this vantage point that he first saw the young bald eagle. Shortly after, he flushed eight ptarmigan from their hiding place among some wind-flattened alder bushes. The ptarmigan still had most of their camouflaging mottled-brown summer feathers, but a few had molted, replacing them with white ones, in anticipation of the coming snow.

Sort of like me, Paul mused, as he watched them whir away, flying low over the rocks and heather: *they're changing their coats, just like I did.* He fondled the new, red, hand-me-down coat he had gotten from the chapel minister.

He smiled and continued climbing, his mind ruminating on events of the past few weeks. A lot had certainly happened.

He now had a permanent boarding home—at least, he hoped it was. He had stayed at the nurse's place for a week, and liked that a lot. She was very nice and kept him fed (as well as clean, with all the hot baths she had him take). Then, one day the principal came and took him to his new home. He had already sort of known the Golodoff family, from when his dad took him visiting in Biorka. It was okay there, but he still liked Nurse Rowan's place best.

School wasn't such a simple matter of *like* or *dislike*, though. What school once meant to him, out in Ichinski, was a pleasant experience: a nice teacher, friends and cousins you grew up with, a small, warm room with everybody together, and being right close to home. But, this kind of school in Biorka wasn't like that at all! It was all very confusing because… well, it wasn't all together; everything that made up a school in Biorka was broken up, and even all the parts were different: the teachers, the building, the kids, food… everything. The teachers were pretty good to him, but having five different ones every day still bothered him; it was hard to adjust to the special demands each made of him. With Miss Richards it had been easy; she was just the same every day.

He was getting used to the building, however. Its enormous size was still disturbing, and he felt uncomfortable to have all that cement and ceiling panels hanging over his head, but it wasn't as bad as before. The gym was scariest at first, but now it was one of his favorite places because, during noon-hour, on especially foul-weather days outside, the students could play in the gym. In truth, it was a loosely controlled free-for-all, since the supervising teachers considered it better for the students to run their energy off there than in the classroom.

By the time Paul and his fellow students finished tearing around and headed to class, his shirt was damp and his hair soaked with perspiration. But, he loved it. They all did, even though it raised the temperature and odor level of the classroom significantly. A smile from the memories lingered on Paul's face as he walked along, then it fell away.

The students were another matter, however. First, there were so many of them. In all his life, Paul had never been around so many bodies in such a small place! All those faces were so unfamiliar to him. There were only 115 in the school, from grades K to 12, but compared to the eleven total pupils at Ichinski, it could just as well have been millions.

But, that wasn't the most disconcerting thing about his fellow students; the worst was how they treated him. Half the time nobody paid much attention to him; he was just left alone. Oh, a few kids talked and played with him—especially one named Moses, whom he liked the most. Kids who did play with him—like Moses—had moved to Biorka within the last five years from other small villages, out on the Aleutian chain of islands or the Alaska Peninsula. They sort of stuck together because of the way the rest of the students treated them: as if village kids were somehow primitive, or something.

It was that other large percentage of students which caused Paul the most discomfort. They didn't want to sit next to him in class; they pushed and tripped him on the playground or gym floor, and called him names. It wasn't just kids his age or younger, either; the worst offenders were often the older kids—even seniors. Paul was pretty scrappy and could at least handle a fight with someone his size, until his opponent's buddies joined in, but when the older kids picked on him, it was much more difficult to stand them off, especially with their much more insulting words and rougher teasing.

For the first week or two, Paul had spent many tearful times after school, sitting alone down under the cannery dock pilings or on the far side of the beach, between some disintegrating fishing boats, trying to understand what was wrong. He would keep going over and over the sequence of events that had resulted in his predicament, but he couldn't think of anything he had done to any of them. It just didn't make sense.

After a while, Paul ceased searching for answers and just stopped asking himself questions; it was getting nowhere. Besides, he was becoming numb to the abuse of his situation. He began to take it all as just the way things were, and became more skilled at dodging encounters. Those he couldn't avoid, he still fought just as strongly, but now he expected them to happen. At least the surprise had gone.

Paul had almost reached the top of the hilltop gap. He was breathing heavily now and sweating. The wind which constantly streamed over the tops of these mountains felt good against his face and body, as it stole underneath his coat and shirt. Losing himself in the last moments of struggle with this approaching physical barrier, Paul felt a new strength in his arms and legs, and his spirits rose. A determined half-smile stole across his face. The air was fresh and cool, and he drank it in through his nose, much as he would drink the clear water melting from the protected snows of the mountain ravines.

The slope gradually became easier, and Paul knew he was almost at the top of the gap. There was very little vegetation left in this place, so exposed was it to the wind, which poured from valley to valley through this funnel. Small clumps of short grass and patches of lichen were all that grew there. The rest of the ground cover was a frost-fractured, weathered, gray rock.

The wind kept up a steady humming sound and, to his

surprise, he could hear a bird singing despite it. He looked to his right, searching, and there at the very top of the gap, standing on a large rock, was a golden-crowned sparrow, singing its heart out. Paul stood frozen by the marvel of this tiny bird, perched in such a forlorn place, torn by the elements, loudly warbling into the void.

Such a brave little fellow, Paul thought, *to stand there like that: all alone and buffeted by the wind, yet still able to be himself and follow what his ancestry urged him to do.*

Paul sat quietly upon the stony heath and remained there, transfixed by the presence and song of the bird, oblivious to the cutting wind buffeting his hair and clothes. The bird's song rose with the wind and drifted out to dissolve in the crystal air of the next valley.

After the sparrow flew away, Paul walked over to an outcropping of basalt, which offered more protection from the wind and had an excellent view of the lagoon and Biorka Bay. From this distance, the town looked small and remote, and Paul liked that. There wasn't much to distract him here, except an occasional bird or insect. Once, a marmot whistled as it stood at the entrance to its den, then disappeared inside. Otherwise, nothing moved nor was heard. Paul silently sat leaning against the basalt, letting his mind wander.

After being immersed in this mountain world for some time, Paul finally noticed that the wind now had a definite chill to it. The sun was lower and being obscured by a light, filmy cloud layer drifting in from the northwest. Paul unfolded his legs from his shelter between two large rocks and stood up, painfully. He had been sitting for too long, he realized, as his joints ached and one leg had fallen asleep.

It was time to return now. Paul knew that, yet he was reluctant to take the first step back to the unfamiliarity and hostility he found in Biorka. *I wish I could stay out here and hunt and fish,* he thought, wistfully. *I could be free again, like that eagle or that little sparrow.* This vision pleased him very much, and he imagined himself roaming over the mountains and valleys, hunting and fishing, living out of a small tent and fending for himself in all ways. *Yeah, that would be great.*

A sudden gust of wind caught Paul off-guard and forced him to take two steps downhill, to keep his balance. With direction and decision thus provided, he reluctantly continued down the hillside, into the gathering darkness. Already, the lights of the town twinkled in the distance and offered a faint suggestion of warmth. He gathered his coat more tightly about him and stumbled numbly onward.

8
Past

Paul

When Paul finally approached the first houses, he started hurrying, since it was almost dinnertime and Mary liked to have everyone there for the Sunday evening meal. She was a wonderful cook and liked to make that meal something special, a fact which Paul greatly appreciated. He imagined he could even smell the food as he first sighted the Golodoffs' house.

Julian Golodoff had built their small, two-bedroom house in 1953, after moving with his wife from Atka. He was attracted to Biorka by the cannery, and the promise of a company boat to use on a share basis. It had worked out well for him, and the family prospered and grew in size. At one time the house held all nine members, with the older children in the extra bedroom and the younger ones in with their parents. After that, the household size decreased as children went out to school or married, until only Peter remained.

Now, Paul shared the bedroom with Peter. This worked out well for the boys since both were accustomed to sharing: Peter with his brothers and Paul with his dad and Uncle James. The boys got along with each other okay; they didn't argue or fight, but neither did they do much of anything together.

When Paul walked into the house that late afternoon, Mary was in the kitchen and Julian was sitting in the living room, reading a newspaper. Julian was a small, stocky man with deep-set crow's feet extending from the corners of his eyes. Being a fisherman, the exposure to wind and sun had bronzed his face and highlighted his facial wrinkles, caused by squinting over the sparkling water and into the beating wind. This emphasized his Aleut features even more, and made him one of the more Native-looking residents of Biorka.

Both he and his wife were born about halfway across the Aleutian Islands on Atka, together with about a fifth of Biorka's population, comprising those whom an outsider would visually consider an Alaskan Native. Most of Biorka's remaining population could not be distinguished from any other middle-class, white people in the Lower 48. To be sure, there might be a few with somewhat rounder faces, lowered eye-folds or slightly darker skin, but those features were easily found elsewhere, too. No, the modern-day Aleuts of Biorka looked like people all over the U.S., with a minority who harkened back to earlier times, in exhibiting an approximation of ancestral Aleut physical features.

Mary was putting on the finishing touches for supper when Paul came in. "Have a good walk?" she asked, as she set another plate on the table.

"Yes, I had a good time," Paul replied, cheerfully. He liked Mary. She was a lot like his grandmother, but without some of the disagreeable traits, like drinking and chewing snuff (he could never get used to that latter habit). Having always fed a large family, Mary enjoyed having Paul there to feed, because he ate about twice as much as anyone else. It was "like having the old family around to feed again," as she put it. She always had snacks for Paul after school and before bedtime, and appreciated his comments on their quality—and quantity. He reminded her of feeding the appetites of some of her older boys, since Peter wasn't much of an eater; that memory made her feel needed again.

"Time to wash up, now; we're about ready to eat. You too," Mary added, looking at Peter, slouched in a chair while paging through a motorcycle magazine.

As both boys trailed off to the bathroom, Mary turned to her husband: "I wonder what he does when he goes out alone like that. Most boys would go with their friends. He doesn't seem to have many, though."

Julian turned his newspaper around and creased it. "Well," he paused and scanned a page, "people here don't care much for those guys over at Ichinski. You know that; you remember what Principal Parkhurst said about having trouble finding somebody to take Paul."

"Yes, but he's only a child. I just don't understand why they would be cruel to a child." Pausing for a moment, Mary continued: "Lots of these people here also came from small villages, and they were kind of backward too when they first got here."

Julian grunted in reply, now absorbed in a newspaper article reporting a fishing trawler with five crew being lost in a storm, south of St. Paul Island in the Bering Sea. Julian read little, but bought the Anchorage paper because he liked to think it kept him up to date on the latest in fishing news.

The boys came back in and supper began.

They were having caribou steak that night, and Paul winced a little. The Golodoffs insisted on certain manners that Paul wasn't used to, and it made eating a task—meat being the worst. He just couldn't get the hang of cutting with his knife in his right hand, while holding the fork properly in the left, and getting the meat to his mouth using the fork, let alone then chewing it slowly! They used tableware out in Ichinski, too, but they used it differently, with much handwork. *Hands are much better at grabbing hold of meat, so why not use them?* Paul wondered. Regardless of the difficulties, however, Paul tried to do as instructed, even though he often had to be reprimanded. He was hungry, after all, and had to eat something!

Other things were new, too: electric lights, the refrigerator and freezer, the gas range, indoor plumbing… and a toilet! He had seen one, of course, and used one a few times before, when visiting his father's friends or relatives in Biorka, but he had never used one daily. By now the newness had worn off, but he still smiled when he flushed the toilet and remembered all those years of running to the outside privy, in the cold of winter, sometimes crying because he got so cold. He would grin in pleasure when he reached into the refrigerator to get an apple or carrot, and remembered what a treat those items were when his dad brought them back from the Biorka stores.

The TV, of course, never failed to amaze Paul with its magic. Even though the satellite feed to the school station and out to the rest of the town was often interrupted by power outages, he never minded having to watch previously recorded programs several times.

Paul thought about these things, as he left the dinner table and settled into a comfortable spot on the living room couch. The good food and warmth of his surroundings made him somewhat sleepy.

Peter turned on the TV and slouched into a chair. As the image formed on the screen, Paul became more alert and sat up, expectantly waiting to be entertained. To Paul's dismay, television reception was poor that Sunday night. They tried a recorded program, but the videotape was simply worn out through three years of use, and the picture was full of lines and squiggles. Finally, Julian turned the set off, cursing the "waste of money," and the house lapsed into silence. Mary continued knitting and Peter went back to his motorcycle magazine. Julian took to cleaning his pipe. Paul just sat there at one end of the couch, blankly staring ahead at the dead set.

Minutes passed. A cheap kitchen clock ticked away.

Paul started looking over the room, as he had done many times before. This time he noticed that something was different. He couldn't place it, but he knew that something was odd about the room. It wasn't the furniture; the same well-used couch and easy chairs were there, with their blankets covering worn spots. Nor was it anything on the coffee or end tables; they were still littered with knick-knacks, lamps and dishes. No, it wasn't there.

The kitchen? No, not there.

On the walls? Well, they were a maze of shelves stacked

with every imaginable object, from family photographs to last year's Christmas tree bulbs. There were cups, saucers and spoons from Mary's collection. Several shelves also held old family heirlooms from earlier Aleut cultural life: a harpoon point, an old slate-stone knife blade, a traditional flat drum, a spear and throwing board, an old…

That was it! It was an old fox trap that was missing.

Paul burst the silence: "Where did it go?"

Mary jumped at the sound of his voice.

"Where did what go?" Julian asked, slightly irritated at being startled.

Noticing everyone's surprised look, Paul replied more quietly: "The fox trap. It was on that shelf." He pointed to the now vacant spot.

"Oh, the history teacher at school wanted to borrow it—for a display or something, I guess."

"We have six traps like that at Ichinski. Some of 'em still work, too. I caught two foxes with 'em last year."

Julian looked at Paul, curiously. "What did you do with them?"

"We used the meat for the dogs, and I dried and tanned the furs. They looked really nice."

"You sell the furs or use them?"

"My dad sold 'em to a tourist at Cold Bay, when he was there. I got five dollars for 'em!" he grinned.

Julian studied the boy's face and grimaced slightly. *That bum Dick Surikov! He even steals from his own son. Hell, I bet he got forty dollars each for those furs!* Shifting his thoughts to the boy again, he asked: "You like that trapping stuff, huh?"

"Oh, yeah," Paul replied enthusiastically, his eyes sparkling, "I really like it. I like to hunt and fish, too. My dad says I make a good Aleut hunter." He added the last proudly.

Julian had put his pipe down while Paul spoke. He now raised it slowly to his mouth and took a couple of quick puffs. Looking at Paul, eagerly leaning forward in his seat, Julian caught a glimpse of his youthful self, also keenly enthused by his prowess at traditional survival skills and especially proud of his grandfather's approving words: "Aleut hunter." How those words had rung in his ears, and how his chest had puffed out! Unconsciously, Julian straightened slightly, and a thrill of sensing the long-lost emotion tingled his spine.

Paul now stood and walked to the shelf where the fox trap had been. Along the back of the shelf were the throwing board and short spear. Oblivious to all around him, he fondled the board, turning it over and admiring its workmanship. He slipped two fingers into the center holes and grasped the board with his hand. Stretching his arm back and positioning the board as if cradling a spear, his eyes met Julian's, who had been intently watching Paul's actions.

The spell of the moment broken, Paul flushed and awkwardly brought his hand down to remove the board and replace it on the shelf. "Uh… my grandfather's is still at Grandma's place. I used to play with it." He returned the board to the shelf.

"Used to be the way we killed seals and otter." Julian paused. Suddenly breaking into a grin, he added: "May have to do it again someday, if the salmon run out!" Then he laughed, and Paul laughed too, in awkward relief.

Julian noticed that Paul had also spied their old gold and red concertina, sitting on a small table among some ceramic figurines. Following a sudden urge, he quickly got up and retrieved it. "You must have heard one of these played, eh, Paul? Bet somebody in your family played?" Almost imploring Paul to confirm his hopes.

Paul's eyes lit up; "Yeah, my grandma used to play one a lot! She's gettin' kinda rusty on it now, but she used to play good."

Julian held the instrument gently in his hands, looking down at it. Mary had silently slipped into the living room and, slightly behind Paul, stood watching her husband. Slowly, Julian slipped his hands into the straps at either end and fingered the buttons. He stopped for a second then, breaking into a slight smile, pulled the ends apart, pushed buttons, squeezed and the brilliant, reedy sounds of the instrument leaped out and filled the room with music.

It was an old Aleut masking song, one which used to be played during Russian Orthodox New Year celebrations. The tempo was quite fast and spirited—one to get everyone immediately involved, foot-tapping or swaying. Julian finished one chorus then, without stopping, called out: "Mary, get your mandolin!"

Mary offered resistance, but with Paul excitedly encouraging and Julian rapidly nodding his head at her, she quickly gave in. Turning around to get the mandolin from their bedroom, she met Peter, grinning widely, with his mother's mandolin in hand. Peter didn't smile that often, but he knew how much his mother loved to play, and the thought of her joy overcame his resistance. Self-consciously smiling in return, Mary turned to join her husband, now sitting on the couch, and was soon picking out an accompaniment to his song.

Paul started to softly sing the Aleut words, then worked up to a full gusto as his hesitancy receded. Peter didn't join in, neither singing nor playing his guitar. Paul knew Peter played fairly well, but guessed that he only knew the popular songs of the day. Instead, he sat slouched back in an easy chair, watching the other three play and sing. Toward the end of the third stanza, Paul ran out of words and mixed up some pronunciation, which sent Julian and Mary into peals of laughter, so they had to stop playing.

Finally, Mary started strumming another masking song, this one at a slightly slower tempo. Julian joined in, but Paul didn't know many words to this one, so he hummed and clapped rhythm. When they finished playing, Julian spoke up: "That's an old one my father taught me. Maybe you don't know it well because it's old, Paul."

He fiddled with the squeeze-box for a moment, trying out different opening phrases, seeking one which would fit the mood of the moment. Striking some solid chords after a short melodic run, Julian looked at Paul and said: "This one was a favorite of my grandmother. She could listen to it for hours." With that brief introduction, Julian launched into a vigorous rendition of "Buffalo Gal", which soon had everybody singing. Even Peter raised his voice to softly contribute.

So the evening went for the next hour, song after song, each one taking the members of the household deeper into the past, when such activity was the only entertainment available before electricity made movies and television possible. At that time, these get-togethers were frequent and provided a time to play and learn the latest hits, as interpreted by returnees from the cities or boarding schools. It was also a time to play and sing the old Aleut songs, keeping the memory of past ages and a dying language alive for just a little longer. The presence of a curious Paul and some lousy TV had returned the family to a form of traditional entertainment and togetherness, which none of them had experienced for some time.

In the middle of one song—an Aleut song of Julian's grandfather's—there was a loud knocking at the door. Mary put down her mandolin to see who it was, while Julian played on and sang his grandfather's song.

When she opened the door, Cal and Lawrence stood there, peering uneasily in at the gathering. Julian looked up sharply from his concentration and, seeing who it was, let the chords die with a wheezy squeeze. The pleasure of the song melted from his face and he stiffened, somewhat.

"Evening, boys," Mary finally spoke up.

"Hi."

"Hullo, Auntie Mary... Julian."

Silence.

With a good-natured grin, Lawrence queried: "Giving Peter some lessons in Atka Aleut, Julian?" Cal stifled a snicker.

Peter blushed a light red and shuffled to his feet. "Nah."

Julian didn't say a word or move. Lawrence's father

frequently teased Julian about his closeness to the old culture, and his darker skin and stocky build. Julian had always quietly taken these humorous but pointed jabs from Benny Gunderson, because if he hadn't it would have only provided fuel for the other fishermen. Benny wasn't from any big place either, but had spent a few years in Kodiak. Besides, he didn't look at all Aleut, just as his son and Cal didn't, either. And, now, here was Lawrence acting just like his father.

"Hey, Peter, you wanna go down to the Sally Ann? I got new tapes in the mail for my stereo." Cal held up his boom-box.

Relieved for an excuse to escape the situation, Peter grabbed his coat. "Yeah, that's alright. You get that one by Death Watch?"

Lawrence answered: "Hey, right! He got some good stuff in. Maybe we can shake the girls with some good sound." Emphasizing the word "good". The three boys laughed at each other, more than was warranted, but the relief from the awkward encounter was welcome.

"I'll be back later, Mom," Peter called, as he tumbled outside with his friends.

"See ya, Julian," Lawrence called out, with apparent innocence. Julian nodded and turned to put his instrument away.

The door banged shut and echoed slightly in the now silent house.

Mary stood facing the door, then slipped quietly back to a task in the kitchen. Paul remained frozen where he was, feeling guilty that he had somehow caused this embarrassing moment for the Golodoffs, yet glad that the joy of the past hour had happened. In the past several weeks, nothing had brought him closer to the memories he had of Ichinski than did this hour of music.

Having laid down his instrument with care, Julian looked at it for a moment, then abruptly turned away and walked to the refrigerator. He reached inside, pulled out a can of beer, and opened it. Snap! He sat down heavily at the table and took a long swig. He stared at the can, rolling it between his hands, then looked up at his wife washing dishes at the sink.

"What the hell," he scowled. "There's nothing left, anyway; all gone now." He took another drink. Mary said nothing, just putting another dish in the rack.

Paul only half-heard and half-understood Julian's words, because he was already back in the music of the masking songs, back at his grandmother's house and back in Ichinski, climbing his mountain.

9
Fire

Catherine

Catherine was outside, hanging the Saturday wash on the clothesline at the back of their house. The sky was overcast as usual, but once in a while a hazy sun filtered through and took off some of the gloom. Several other women were also out hanging clothes and, in short order, the empty lots running along behind the houses were bedecked with clothes, strung on a wild array of lines.

Frequently, the lines were too weighed down and sagged deeply. So, for added support, poles, branches, driftwood and even old boat oars propped up the sagging line. The effect of this was that the loaded lines flopped from side to side at the whim of the frequent gusts which blew. On that day, Catherine stood out amidst these suspended, flopping clotheslines, adding her family's contribution.

Her mother was just bringing out another load of clothes when one of the fellow hangers called out: "Where's that smoke coming from?"

Catherine and her mother looked up, to see a thin line of smoke coming from what appeared to be the end of the cannery buildings. "Looks like somebody's burning trash.

They better be careful around those buildings," Catherine's mother replied.

Indeed, it did look like about enough smoke for a trash fire, such as the one the company often burnt in their large trash burner—except that the burner was located at the end of some other buildings. As they watched, the smoke noticeably increased.

"I don't know," another neighbor commented; "that doesn't look right to me. Too much smoke."

Just then, two kids rode by on their bicycles from that direction, pumping as hard as they could and yelling: "The cannery's on fire!"

Catherine dropped the clothes-pins she was holding and clapped her hands to her face. Without speaking, her mother put down the basket of clothes. Drying her hands on her apron, she walked to the closest boardwalk and toward the cannery. Catherine immediately started walking, too, as did the other women. By the time they reached the main boardwalk, other people had also noticed the fire and were hurrying silently in that direction. Suddenly, a cloud of black smoke belched out of a rooftop ventilator on the storage warehouse, affirming the townspeople's fears and bringing a muffled chorus of exclamations.

There had never been a cannery fire in Biorka, but it wasn't all that uncommon an occurrence in Alaska. The cannery in King Cove burnt the previous year, and two years before that one in Chignik. Of course, there had been some fires in town, such as when the cannery boiler blew up, and the year the men's dorm burnt down, but never the main buildings of the cannery itself.

As they approached the first building, they saw flames flitting out at the roofline. Catherine could now see clearly where the fire was: the north end of the storage warehouse was where it had started—it had begun inside and was just now showing its menacing face outside the building. Men were at work trying to open the doors at that end, but the heat and smoke were already too much for sustained attempts.

A fire hose was hooked up from the bunkhouse, but the little stream directed through the opened doors was clearly insufficient. Other hoses were dragged out and attached to the waterline. As it turned out, though, only one short line had water in it; the other primary lines were empty, having been drained two weeks ago, so the pipes wouldn't freeze during the winter. Moreover, the main valves were chained and locked. While the men stood helpless, nozzles in hand and watching the fire grow, a frantic search was underway to find the keys.

Catherine watched with the growing crowd of spectators, as the coating on the sheet-metal buildings caught fire from the intense heat, and burnt brilliantly with an orange, blue-tinged flame.

Someone shouted: "Over here! It's spreading underneath!" The crowd moved as one body to look where the man pointed. He was right: looking underneath, at the three-foot space separating the building foundation from the earth, they could see yellow flames creeping steadily outward from beneath the warehouse, eating their way along the supporting timbers to the next building. The fire had burnt through the warehouse floor and was spreading outward, through the creosote-treated timbers which made up the pilings and flooring foundation of the cannery buildings. It provided excellent fuel, and the fire was insidiously using that advantage.

"That's it," someone announced; "there's no way to stop it now! It'll take the whole thing."

Catherine could see that the man was probably right: this was it; it was all over. As she watched the spreading fire, Catherine thought, half-amused: *At least I maybe won't get stuck working in that hole next summer now, after I graduate!* She smiled slightly at the thought of being freed from those long hours and endless rows of salmon coming at her, but the smile faded rapidly.

Yeah, but what will I do then? There's not much else to do in this place, but work in the cannery—except get married and raise kids! Repulsed by that image, she turned with increased concern to the shouts of men running forward with hoses.

The keys were found and water turned on. Nothing happened for a moment or two. Finally, water started to trickle and then stream from the hoses. One hose immediately burst from the pressure, rotten from lying folded for so many years. The men—cannery workers, fishermen, teachers—all worked hard to hose down the burning building, but the fire was well advanced and spreading rapidly. Soon, the can shop and web house had smoke wafting, then pouring out of their roof ventilators. Flames quickly followed.

By now, large cylinders of propane, which had been stored in the warehouse, were exploding, making it especially dangerous to be near the building. Each time one blew up there was a sharp report and a hollow ringing of metal, as the force of the blast blew sections of the roof twisting into the air, as a cylinder punched through. Once, four cylinders went off together, bursting out through the warehouse wall and into the web house, where nets and other fishing gear were stored.

A voice exclaimed, "The gas shop!" as if in sudden memory of its existence. "Let's get that stuff out of there!"

The crowd rushed from the back around to the front wharf side. Farther up the wharf, fork-lift tractors were already scooting in and out of the can shop through the increasingly heavy smoke, taking pallet-loads of canned salmon out to the far sea end of the piers. Pitching in to likewise save some of the oil products stored in the gas shop, and to deprive the fire of added fuel, the crowd started a bucket-brigade of children, women and men, rolling barrels of fuel and passing cases of oil out to the end of the wharf. Soon, it was necessary to go deeper into the building to reach the goods.

Already, the web house next door was burning fiercely, and the roaring sound of the conflagration a few feet away was chilling to those who penetrated deep into the gas shop. Shortly, a loud explosion ripped off a front section of the web house wall and flames leaped into the air, sending the crowd scurrying back along the wharf, to where the oil goods had been dumped. It was now clear that any further effort to save the gas shop—or any other building—was futile.

Pam and Jim Irving stood away from the wharf, panting slightly from the rush of work, and looked back at the fire, now engulfing the building they had been inside just a few minutes before. Julian Golodoff, who had been standing beside them, turned as if to leave.

"Looks like that's it," Jim volunteered.

"Yup, not much left now," Julian replied, as he turned to stay, and wiped his oil- and charcoal-smudged hands on a back-pocket handkerchief.

Like other people who had handled the fuel drums and other items, the Irvings' clothes and shoes were covered with oily dirt. They stood in silence as the flames leaped higher and lit their faces. Soon it became too hot to stay and, with resignation, they turned to leave.

But, what they now saw confused them greatly.

A number of the townspeople were busily carrying off cases of oil products to load onto their pickups, motorcycles or three-wheelers. Some pickups were already driving off with fifty-gallon drums of gas and oil, so overloaded that the rear bumpers dragged. What had previously been a very serious scene had suddenly turned into a carnival atmosphere, as the opportunists turned to take whatever they could, now that it was hopeless to stop the fire.

"I don't get it," Jim muttered, in dismay. "Don't they realize that they're helping destroy the only thing that makes it possible for them to live here?"

Pam only shrugged her shoulders. "Let's go."

As the three of them walked down the road, an overloaded pickup slowly bounced past. In the back were Cal and Lawrence, grinning broadly. Lawrence waved to them and called: "Some fire, eh?"

"Yup, some fire," Jim agreed.

"Second load!" Lawrence announced, proudly. "This one's for Cal's dad." Cal beamed even more.

As the truck rumbled off, two motorcycles went by, each with two cases of oil tied on the back. A three-wheeler then went by, even more loaded down. The driver, an older man in his fifties, nodded nonchalantly and drove on. Jim acknowledged the nod, then shook his head, as they walked on through the procession of loaded vehicles.

Catherine and Paul had also been at the wharf, helping to move the oil. The two ended up working next to each other, and now that the fire finally forced a halt to their efforts, they stood watching the fruit of their labor being stolen: by the fire behind them and the scavengers in front, both consuming that which was not rightfully theirs. Catherine and Paul were conflicted in their emotions. Neither spoke a word, but both were conscious of the feelings the other had.

The fire raged more intensely now. More vehicles arrived and people swarmed over the pile of goods.

Without looking at Catherine, Paul stated, softly: "It isn't right, is it?" He stood there, staring ahead.

Catherine glanced down at the thin figure beside her. Paul's new red coat was smudged with oil and dirt. His tousled black hair jutted out from a green cap, and his face was streaked where he had wiped his nose on the back of an oil-stained hand. She said nothing at first, then shrugged; "No, it isn't."

At that moment her father, Gene Cheripanof, drove up with a neighbor in his battered old Dodge pickup. A chorus of salutations greeted Gene's arrival and, after a few jokes and laughs, he and his neighbor started loading their truck. Once, when he glanced around he saw Catherine—at least, she thought he had—but he never broke his rhythm of work.

Somehow, Catherine felt uneasy about all this, especially her father being there, loading up with the rest of the men. She agreed with Paul that it wasn't right; however, she knew that it would save money for the family, having extra oil and fuel for the boat. *Yes, it wasn't theirs, but wasn't the cannery getting rich off of the fishermen? And didn't her father catch fish for the cannery?* She debated, internally: *True, but he also got paid for the fish.* It was extremely confusing, as though her head and heart were telling her to believe opposing things.

At that moment, Cal and Lawrence showed up to help Lawrence's dad load his truck. The obvious enthusiasm with which they threw themselves into the job, and their grinning festive faces, suddenly sickened Catherine. She'd had enough. Without a word, she turned down the road and headed back.

Ahead of her, Julian Golodoff was slowly walking along, empty-handed, giving an occasional nod to those passing by. Following behind Catherine, Paul spied Julian and ran past her, to abruptly stop and walk along at his side. Paul glanced up at Julian, his face serious, then settled into Julian's pace.

After it was fully dark, a Coast Guard cutter tied up to the wharf to lend aid. By then, though, little could be done: the web house, warehouse and gas shop had collapsed, and the can shop had only two walls standing. Flames still lit up the town and hillside, as the fire continued to finish consuming what it had claimed. It was under control from spreading now, but what it owned was almost everything.

When Catherine finally left the scene for good, most of the other people were on their way, too. As they walked along the boardwalk, Catherine couldn't help overhearing their conversations about the fire and the losses many of them had sustained—not only from equipment stored in the buildings, but also from the cargo that a freighter had deposited just the day before. The uncertainty and confusion of the event lent an air of tenseness to the quick backward glances people gave, as they straggled along toward home. There was no wind, and the sounds of the fire as it crackled and timbers crashing carried far over the water and town.

Almost at home, Catherine took a final look at the fire, now more a glowing hotbed of coals, sending sparks into the air, than the flaming inferno it had once been. The floodlights of the Coast Guard ship shone a brilliant white against the reddish glow of the fire, as the crew snaked long hoses out of the ship, like tentacles claiming the remaining wharves. Here and there an arching stream of water could be seen, as it was directed on a flare-up blaze.

Well, Catherine concluded, *it's theirs now; it's theirs for the night. Then, tomorrow it will again be ours: ashes, burnt hopes and an uncertain future.*

Catherine felt exhausted. She pushed the gate open and went up the house steps, letting the gate close with a sharp bang.

Like nearly everyone in the town, Catherine frequently returned later, drawn by the magnetism of the fire.

10
Aftermath

Cal

The next day, the sun rose slowly through the early morning mist, hanging over the lower elevations of the hillside. Decaying vegetation on the heather warmed to the sun and steamed, sending tendrils of moisture up to the morning light. The night had been cold, but despite that warning of the coming winter, it promised to be a decent day—except when looking toward the ruins of the cannery.

In that space there now stretched a gray, ashen wasteland of smoldering timbers and red, rusted metal. Only the can shop was distinguishable, now reduced to a maze of charred machinery, which stood amidst the burnt beams and ashes like armed giants frozen in time, its pipes bent into pretzel forms by the intense heat. Where the huge, shiny buildings once stood, there was now one very large garbage heap.

Cal was up early that morning. He and his dad had just finished securing the *Panof* to a piling, after having motored over from the boat harbor. They slowly climbed the ladder to the top of the wharf.

Where the cannery buildings had once overshadowed the

wharf, there were now only space and a clear sky. Even the end of the lagoon and Mount Daniels were visible in the distance, above the rubble. Cal's father let out a low whistle and, shaking his head, ambled over to a group of fishermen. Cal followed close by.

"Morning, Gregory," several voices welcomed.

Gregory nodded in acknowledgment. "Holy, what a mess!" he muttered, as he surveyed the ruins. Murmurs of agreement came from the men, and all took another long look at the scene.

"You lose much, Greg?" It was Benny Gunderson.

"Well, several thousand, I figure." He paused. "But, the thing that hurts most was the new hydraulic hoses and controls I had made for the winch controls." He was referring to the winches which operated his seine net lines on the *Panof*. "It takes two or three good weeks of work putting that in, and it'll be colder than hell to work on by the time another set gets here in February!" Heads shook in dismay.

"I guess Al Olson about got wiped out: whole year's order of food, I hear," another man offered.

"Yeah, he had tough luck with his boat this summer, too; didn't get much fishin' time in," Benny commented.

"Well, if he'd get his head out of the bottle, he'd catch a few fish," commented a lean man, wearing a well-used, yellow rain slicker.

"You should talk!" a voice from the other side of the wharf called out. A stocky man wearing a red mackinaw and navy watch-cap strode up to the group, grinning widely. "You almost sent the *Betty G* to the bottom last summer, because you caught more bottles than fish!" As the lean man's face went sour, the other men guffawed loudly at the crack, and welcomed Sam Livengood into the circle.

Sam was foreman of the cannery and, though he was an outsider, he was generally respected and actually well-liked by the fishermen, primarily because of his quick wit and jovial nature. It was hard for anybody to stay mad at him for long, and the man who was the butt of his wisecrack quickly softened up, because he knew that what Sam had said was true. Sam always hit the nail on the head squarely, but with humor.

After the laughter, the men settled down to a more somber mood. The silence of the place, with that special ingredient that disaster always adds, brought their minds again to the reality of the day.

Sam scanned slowly from one end of the smoldering junk heap to the other. "Damn! What a mess!" He shook his head in disbelief and weariness. Several men muttered agreement.

"What you fellows gonna do now? You gonna build 'er up again, I guess, eh? Not much choice." Benny tried to make his question into a statement, to allay his fears, shared by many others, that perhaps Arctic Queen wouldn't rebuild, and instead would just leave the ruins and expand facilities elsewhere.

Suspicion about the company's motives and resentment of the town's dependency always lay just under the surface. Rarely did anyone talk openly in terms of the cannery versus the community. They didn't quite talk of "us" against "them"; it was usually voiced in specific gripes, by individuals, about the cannery: they complained about getting a bum deal on the cannery boat contract that season, or that the company store prices were too high. They complained that their daughter should have been paid more for work on the line, or that the line supervisor was too busy and too bossy. Benny asked his question hoping to be right about rebuilding, but he also put a bite into it by assuming the company had no choice.

Sam was no fool, and picked up the slant to Benny's question. Caught as he was between the community and the cannery, since he was employed by the latter, yet had married a local woman and settled in Biorka, Sam still resented the way the fishermen pushed it all off onto the cannery.

Drawing a deep breath and pausing a moment for effect, Sam started: "Well, I don't know. Of course, the boss hasn't had much time to do any talkin', with the office in Seattle, so he probably isn't too sure about what's gonna happen. Still, a lot of the decision will be his, because he's closest to the situation here." Sam quickly scanned the men's faces, out of the corner of his eye. He continued: "It's pretty late to get this stuff cleaned up and a new building started for next summer, let alone replace the machinery. Some of that equipment is pretty tough to replace; they don't even make half of it anymore. We'd need to have most of it custom-made, unless some of this can be repaired."

Silence.

"I don't know. Maybe they won't want to rebuild. I guess we'll have to wait and see."

Gregory Larsen spoke up, rather sharply: "Christ, Sam! The company can't leave everybody stranded here! My dad only came here because the cannery was opening up, and that's the only reason. Holy, without the cannery, there wouldn't be any town here!" he stated, emphatically.

Cal looked at his father. He had never seen him so outspoken. Gregory rarely said much in a conversation and, if he did, it was usually without emotion. Cal was astonished. Then, it occurred to him: *What would our family do if the cannery didn't rebuild?*

Sam's voice broke in on Cal's thoughts: "Now, don't get me wrong, I said I didn't know exactly what was going to happen; I'm just guessing. Besides, the crab processing is still going—those buildings weren't touched—and reds and tanners have been good for several years now; Arctic Queen won't want to abandon that. Everybody's just gonna have to wait a while," he concluded.

One of the Coast Guard officers was heading over to the group. "Mr. Livengood," he called, "I think we're about finished now. Would you come over for a moment, please?"

The officer waited for Sam, then they both started walking down the wharf, to the ship. "Later, boys," Sam called out. They gave a few nods in reply.

The men turned again to face the ruin and each other.

"Well?" someone offered.

"Didn't give us much to go on, did he?" another man retorted. Several shook their heads.

"Just like Arctic Queen," the lean man in the yellow slicker added: "get us good and in debt to them, then foreclose and pull out."

"Now, Sam didn't say that for sure; he said he didn't

know," Benny countered. "I guess we'll just have to wait, as he said."

The men stood there for a few minutes more, then began to disband, some going back to their boats and work, while others walked around to survey the extent of the damage and poke around a little. Cal was left standing alone.

He glanced up at the leaden sky and out at the oily-smooth sea swells. Three gulls were squawking over a large piece of cracked crab, which had slipped through the processing line into the water. Cal stared down at them. Their lively, raucous scrapping seemed very out of place with the seriousness of the situation. They don't even notice, he thought; nothing has happened, as far as they're concerned. With a flourish of anger, he kicked a charred board off the dock and into their midst, raising the clamor and flapping to a higher pitch.

As Cal climbed back down the ladder to finish his job on the boat, the anger receded and an uneasy feeling swept in. For the first time in his life, Cal's future was overshadowed by doubt, from questions forced upon him by the fire. *What if the cannery isn't rebuilt?* What would his dad do? What would *he* do? Fishing was all Cal had ever considered—following in his father's footsteps. There wasn't much of anything else a man could work at in Biorka, anyway. If you were a fisherman, you were one of the guys, and if you captained a boat, you were respected. Who could ask for more?

These thoughts roiled in Cal's mind, as he worked at his task onboard. Somehow, though, they wouldn't straighten themselves out into a neat, understandable package. And, to complicate matters, a new one popped in: he remembered the incident last year when Campbell, the business teacher, gave his class this impassioned speech about thinking of their future and looking over the available choices. At that time, the idea of "something else" was so foreign to Cal that it never sank in; he couldn't conceive of "something else". Now, however, those words started to make sense. He was beginning to understand how there might need to be something else, now that the fire had shaken his security.

He turned around and looked for his father. At first, Cal didn't see him, then he heard a noise in the pilothouse. Walking forward, he saw the bulk of his father bent over on his knees, working on some controls. Cal stepped inside and waited.

His dad said nothing; he either didn't hear Cal or ignored him. Finally, Cal spoke up: "Uh, Pop?"

No answer, just a small sound of straining, as his father struggled to reach a hidden wire.

"Whatcha think they're gonna do about the cannery?" Cal waited, but again no answer came. *He must have heard me,* Cal thought, anxiously.

"I mean, you think they're gonna rebuild it?" Cal waited longer this time.

Finally, with a small sound of success, and clasping the end of a broken electrical wire in his right hand, Gregory Larsen lifted himself slightly from his awkward, bent position and looked up at his son's questioning face. "Hell, I don't know, Cal. That's *their* business. The fish are out there in the sea and we go catch 'em—that's *our* business. Nothin' else we can do."

He then turned to look at the wire in his hand and, remembering where he figured the loose terminal was, set about his task again.

Cal blankly stared at his father's back, as he worked at the controls. After a moment, he turned, picked up the rope again and numbly started working. With a gnawing in his stomach and a feeling that the tall pilings surrounding the boat were closing in on him, Cal felt more alone than ever before in his life. Seeking solace in his work, he struggled furiously with his rope splices, as the boat rocked gently in the cradle of the piers, above which the ashen ruins of the cannery still smoldered.

11
Security

Catherine

The cannery fire had also disrupted Catherine's sense of security.

She had never enjoyed working at the cannery. It was always cold, messy work and the odor was sometimes hard to get rid of. Her long, rubberized apron and knee-high boots always stank; it wasn't worth it to do anything more than just hose them off each day. So, from as soon as she got into her gear until she stepped out of it, the odor and awareness of not being entirely clean stayed with her all day.

Sometimes, the days were rather long, too; twelve to fourteen hours was not uncommon. When the fish were unloaded from the boats, they had to either be packed or let spoil, since storage space was limited, even with an ice-house at the cannery. The breaks for snacks and coffee or meals were the times Catherine looked forward to. It seemed that was all she lived for on the long days.

Her mind and body were numb from the repetitious actions, which dragged on hour after hour. It did little good to try to think about anything specific, because she just couldn't overcome the stupefying rhythmic power of the job and the machines. At the end of the day, she was usually exhausted and fell into bed shortly after eating. It wasn't much of a life, and she never thought she would miss it.

However, now that the fire had carried away the possibility of her repeating that job next summer, a black cloud of uncertainty enveloped her. Summer was now an enormous, gaping hole in the yearly wheel of seasons and, day by day, Catherine felt herself sliding around that wheel, toward the void. As the weeks went by and Christmas vacation approached, she increasingly found herself occupied with thoughts of the cannery and the future.

One day, a week before vacation, Catherine was in her social studies class, half-listening to Mrs. Irving, as usual. This time, however, she was roused out of her mulling mind by something Mrs. Irving said. No, it wasn't something she had said—more how she had said it.

For the past week, the class had been covering the legal rights of minority groups in the U.S., and historical events connected with African Americans and Native Americans. When she pointed out that Aleuts were a minority group, too, Catherine and the rest of the class could hardly grasp the idea of them being considered as something different from other people. Truthfully, few in the class had any idea of what "other people" were, since they traveled very infrequently outside Biorka.

However, on this day Mrs. Irving additionally brought up the fact that, although they made up one-half of the U.S. population, women were considered a minority, because they were also denied various rights throughout history. She then listed off a number of these rights, such as voting, employment, social standing, education and many others.

Mrs. Irving could see from the looks on the students' faces that she wasn't getting very far, especially with the boys, who were smirking. Yet, she could see that she caught the attention of some of the girls, so she tried a more direct approach.

"What choices do you girls have for you here in Biorka? What are you going to do after you graduate? What kind of future can you expect?" She paused to look at the class, then walked to the chalkboard. "Let's list some possibilities on the board. What is the most common thing girls do after they graduate or quit school?" She looked around the class.

A husky voice called out: "Get married!" It was Cal, slouched back in his chair and grinning slightly, obviously pleased with his crack, since it got a loud response from the rest of the boys.

"Well, okay; that's one possibility. I don't see many of you girls laughing about it, though. Is marriage a choice or is it the only thing available? How about it, girls?"

No one said anything for a moment, then Sharon Larsen, a cousin of Cal's, spoke up. "I'm gonna get married 'cause I want to," she announced, loudly.

A few in the class snickered. It was well known that she would marry Fred Odegaard, Mark's older brother. They were seen walking hand in hand together everywhere, and they weren't hesitant about showing their affection in public—which irritated some older folks.

"Okay," Mrs. Irving broke in, "you feel you have a choice then?"

"Yes!" was the tart reply.

"What did you choose between, then?" Mrs. Irving pressed.

"Being an old maid!" Lawrence cracked. This brought the house down.

"Shut up, you stupid..." Sharon went on to attack Lawrence with a barrage of curses.

Mrs. Irving quickly stepped in to stop the argument and keep the discussion going. "Hold it! Hold it! Let's get back on track. Sharon considers herself to have a choice, and that's her right. Maybe she could tell us about it."

Sharon was still furious. "I'm gonna get married 'cause I want to. My mom's done okay: she married a good fisherman, and they got their own boat and house and truck and... and... they're both happy. So, I don't see nothin' wrong with it."

Catherine, in the meantime, had been watching the discussion intensely, and found herself strangely put off by Sharon's arrogant, definite behavior. She seemed so sure of it all.

"Okay. Good." Mrs. Irving wanted to get on. "Let's put marriage and family on the board as a choice." She wrote it down and turned back to the class. "Now, what else is there?"

There was a pause, as the class shifted gears from the uproar to a more serious atmosphere.

Finally, a soft voice spoke: "Well, there used to be the cannery, but now it's gone." It was Catherine speaking.

"Yes, it's gone, but there is still work at the crab plant," Mrs. Irving added.

"But," Catherine objected, "the crab plant takes women

only on the packing line, and there's just ten on it. Most of those are older women who have worked there for a long time. It's hard to break into."

"Well, the salmon cannery will probably be rebuilt."

"Yeah, maybe." Catherine paused, then, with a greater sense of urgency, pressed on: "But, that will be a year or two from now; they take so long to get anything done out here. So, what are we supposed to work at until then?"'

Mrs. Irving watched Catherine's face carefully, and saw the anguish increase as she spoke. "The fire truly limits the choices for some of you, doesn't it? How many of you girls were planning on working in the cannery next summer?"

Seven hands out of eight went up.

"Now what will you do?" She let the question stand.

Bernice Kuzakin, a quiet girl with brown hair and delicate features, slowly raised her hand. "I can crew on my dad's boat," she said, matter-of-factly. Everyone turned around.

"You're crazy," one boy chuckled.

Mrs. Irving took advantage of the moment: "Why can't she? What's wrong with a girl fishing on a boat?"

"She wouldn't know what to do," the boys piped up; "it'd be too hard'a work."

"I already know what to do," Bernice countered, "and the work isn't always hard, either."

"How would you know?" sneered one boy.

"Because I've done it before—have for the last two summers. My dad pays me a regular crew's percentage, and I do everything the regular crew does."

Everyone was silent.

"Well," Mrs. Irving began, "it looks like there is another possibility we can put on the board."

After she had written it down, she turned to the class. "Remember, class, just because someone has never done a particular activity before doesn't mean they can't learn it. That's what minority discrimination is all about: women haven't tried a lot of jobs because it was assumed they couldn't do them. Now, after women have tried new kinds of jobs and found they can do them, a lot more jobs are open to them." She paused. "What else is there in Biorka?"

Storekeeper, school custodian and secretary were brought up, and the list seemed to be at its end. Mrs. Irving pointed out that there weren't that many openings for any of these occupations in the town, since there was only one school, three stores and two offices. The students were stumped, and seemed to be trying hard to think of something else.

Mrs. Irving decided to change the perspective. "Now, remember, we're talking about choices that are open to you girls anywhere. We've only discussed the choices in Biorka so far. What other choices are there?"

No one answered. Nobody seemed to understand her question.

Finally, from the back of the room, Alice Kuzakin boomed out: "Leave this place!"

It was no secret that Alice wasn't crazy about Biorka, since it had been the scene of two unsuccessful attempts at marriage by her mother, and each time Alice was sent back and forth from Biorka to Anchorage. She was always making comments about what a dull place Biorka was, and what she used to be able to do in Anchorage for excitement. Her comment was no surprise.

Alice's statement, however, shifted the focus of the discussion, and this was what Mrs. Irving had been waiting for. "Alright, going elsewhere is another choice. If you went out, what kinds of choices would you have?"

The other students still hadn't shifted their thinking and weren't quite adjusted to the concept of leaving Biorka. Not that they were unfamiliar with the idea, since people were frequently going in and out, but few of the students had ever lived Outside, and never had they thought of themselves leaving for good.

"Okay, Alice, what would you do if you left?"

Alice hesitated, then spoke out: "I'd go out Anchorage, get a job and live in an apartment."

"Do you think you could find a job?"

"Oh, yeah! There are lots of jobs in stores, restaurants and offices. My mom has a good job in a lounge, and I have a lot of girlfriends my age who have good jobs."

Catherine had been watching Alice in wonder. She knew Alice had been quite unhappy since she returned to Biorka this time, and had talked a lot about how she didn't like living with her aunt, how the boys here were backward and so on. However, Catherine hadn't put the parts together and now realized that Alice was itching to get back to Anchorage. The idea of leaving here by herself, getting a job and living in an apartment… it was all too much for Catherine to absorb. So, when one student asked Alice where she thought she would stay, Catherine waited anxiously for her to answer.

"I'd get an apartment with some other girls, or by myself," she added, gaining more courage. "That's the way you live out there. Holy, it isn't like here, where you have to live with your parents or some relative, and have them watch you all the time. You can do stuff you want to and earn money for yourself. You don't have to beg it off your folks or some guy you married!" Definitely pleased with her little speech, Alice settled her stout frame back into her chair and flashed her black eyes about the classroom, waiting for an attack from the boys.

Mrs. Irving was rather surprised at the venom in Alice's comments and knew that it was liable to get some reaction from the boys.

"Okay, let's get it down on the board, like this," she stepped to the chalkboard: "let's break your choices down, under the categories of those possible if you stay in Biorka and those possible if you leave Biorka. Now, if you leave Biorka you can work at a job, or... what?"

Slowly, Ruth Dudren raised her hand.

"Yes, Ruth?"

"You could go to school, or something," Ruth answered.

"Okay, that's another choice. You could go to someplace like the business schools in Anchorage or Fairbanks, or to a University of Alaska community branch for two years, or even to one of the universities, to get a four-year degree. I'd like to get more into all that later; right now, I just want to point out that, by choosing to leave Biorka, it's possible to either get a job or to go on for more training, to get a better job."

"Hey, you left one out," a boy offered.

"What's that?"

"They could still get married... to a guy on the Outside!" The boys had a laugh about that.

Smiling and going along with the crack, Mrs. Irving agreed: "Yes, that is another choice." Gaining control of the conversation's direction again, she added: "It would certainly open up a lot of choices as to the specific type of role a wife could have: store employee, business owner, home services professional, member of service clubs, a partner in the husband's business, or a teacher... like me. There are a lot of things a wife can do, besides cook and raise children." Her point seemed well taken, since the class remained quiet.

Mrs. Irving had just enough time to take advantage of the silent class to add, "We'll take this up later and examine the choices more closely," before the bell rang and the students erupted into the hallway.

Outside, Catherine caught up to Alice and Ruth. The three of them walked down the hall together without speaking.

Finally, Ruth broke the spell: "You sure sounded like you meant what you said, Alice."

"Of course I did!" She flashed a threatening look toward Ruth. Alice was solidly built and also taller than Ruth, so she involuntarily jumped when Alice spoke so sharply. "Cripes, you think I'd ever marry one of those creeps in that class and live here? Ho, all they think women are good for is to have babies and cook for them. I'll be damned if I'll get stuck in that trap, like my mother did. Every time she got married, the guy saddled her with a couple more kids and drank up all the food money, then beat her 'cause he didn't like what he got to eat." She caught her breath. "Boy, none of that for me. I want to be free and take care of myself."

The girls arrived at their lockers and stopped to get books for the next class. Alice had a different one, so she left while Ruth and Catherine walked on.

"Do you think she'll go through with it? I mean, go get a job and all?" Catherine asked.

Ruth looked at Catherine. "She sounded pretty determined about it, didn't she?"

"I don't know whether I could ever do that," Catherine replied. "I'd be scared to be by myself, with strangers all around."

"Me too," Ruth agreed. "But, if somebody you knew was along—like... well... you, it'd be a lot easier."

When Ruth said "you" Catherine froze. The brief flash she had of herself in that situation was terrifying.

Ruth turned to her wide-eyed, ashen-faced companion. "Why, Catherine," she said, grabbing Catherine's arm, and burst out laughing, "I joke! I'm just talking."

Catherine quickly regained control and laughed, too, realizing how ridiculous she must have looked, and the two girls leaned on each other for support.

It was almost time for their consumer math class, and they hurried on down the hall, still chuckling over the incident.

They found their seats and sat down. Then, with a knowing look at each other, they broke into giggles again. Mr. Campbell warned the girls about their behavior, and they settled into the routine.

Halfway through class, Ruth passed a note to Catherine. Ruth had her head on her desk, turned expectantly toward her, as Catherine picked the note up off the floor, where it was dropped. She glanced up at Ruth, then read the note:

"What if we did go out and get an apartment together in Anchorage?"

Catherine's eyes were glued to the paper. She read it again and again, as if trying to make the meaning of the words somehow sink in better. Finally, Catherine turned to face Ruth. Ruth still had her strange look, and Catherine could only stare back, blank and uncomprehending. *What is Ruth thinking? Why Anchorage? To do what?*

Mr. Campbell's voice rudely brought them both back to the class. Ruth gave Catherine a wink and, with a sparkle in her eyes, turned her face back to the front of the room.

Catherine cornered Ruth after school, later that day, and demanded to know what she was up to. Ruth responded that she'd just had this great brainstorm about the two of them going out to college and rooming together. Catherine was better prepared for the unexpected this time.

"Now, where did you get that idea?" Catherine knew her friend well and was familiar with other wild schemes of hers.

"Nowhere," Ruth protested. "I mean, from no one person, exactly. You know, Laura and Boots went out last year, and my sister did, too, after she graduated. It's nothing new, after all," she emphasized.

This was true. Over the years, there had always been a few

Biorka young people who went to college, somewhere in Alaska, to either state-supported or Church-supported ones. A few even went out of state, to Washington or Oregon, or technical schools for Native Americans in Nebraska or New Mexico, for example. However, the problems of adjustment were the same in-state or out, and few students could make the change easily. Most eventually returned home.

"Yes, but Laura and Boots only stayed until Christmas vacation, then came home," Catherine protested. "They were so homesick they had a four-hundred dollar phone bill calling home! It's silly to go put yourself in a spot where you'll do that."

"Yeah, but it doesn't have to be that way. Laura and Boots were chicken; they were both Mamma's little pets," Ruth scoffed, imitating mannerisms of the two. "My sister, Georgiana, really liked it at Fairbanks. She had a great time."

"So, how come she came back home?"

"Well," Ruth faltered for a moment, then went on, "she needed to work and make some more money. She met Gill, too: that guy from Kodiak. When he left her, she was broken up about that for a while. But Georgiana went back for another year." Ruth brightened. "She tried, at least, and now she works pretty steady at an office in Anchorage."

"But, does she like it?" Catherine emphasized.

"Ask her yourself. She's coming home for Christmas."

It wasn't quite the satisfying answer from Ruth that Catherine wanted, but at least now she knew what Ruth was thinking. Going off to school somewhere, the two of them, alone... the thought of it gave Catherine the chills. Yet, there was something about the idea that intrigued her. After all, what was she going to do after graduation?

Throughout Christmas vacation, this final thought continually tormented her.

12
Home

Paul

Paul was waiting expectantly for Christmas vacation to come, since he would go back to Ichinski for ten days. But, as no word came from his dad, his spirits sank lower each day. Increasingly, the sense of being abandoned crept over him: abandoned amongst strangers.

Yes, he had adjusted to the extent of forming a small niche of patterned daily activity in the life of the community, but he still felt like a foreigner. And, now that he had shifted his focus over to the expectation of leaving, he had temporarily cut even those ties of daily activity and stood on the edge of the community—a voluntary outcast, waiting to be picked up and rescued. But, the rescue was slow in coming.

Finally, the day before Christmas, word came via a passing fishing boat that Paul was to walk across the peninsula and meet his dad on the other side. The sea was too rough to take a skiff around the point. Since it was well into the morning that day, Paul had to be quick. He said a brief goodbye to the Golodoffs and set off along the lagoon, toward the hills.

Paul made good time, and in four hours could see a small skiff drawn up on the beach. He waved and shouted, and in ten minutes was standing alongside, but no one was there. Paul stared at the skiff again, a feeling of panic rising within. Yes, this is my dad's boat, alright, he affirmed, as he glanced over its contents. But, where was his dad?

Something else looked strange, too: everything was thrown inside hurriedly, and not neatly shipshape, like his dad usually left it—even when he'd been drinking. Maybe something had happened to him in the village… or here.

Paul started examining the ground for tracks. Sure enough, there they were: two sets, running from the boat; two people. Now Paul became scared. Suppose a big brownie had surprised his father and companion? Those bears could move so fast it was unbelievable. Absorbed in his panicked thoughts as he was, Paul did not notice the movement on the bluff above him.

Surprised by a sound above, Paul whirled about. His heart had almost stopped by the time he realized what it was. With great relief, he shouted and waved to his dad and Uncle James, at the top of the bluff.

They were each dragging something behind them, through the tall grass, and they had rifles slung across their backs. Paul's father pulled his object halfway over the brink of the bluff, and Paul could see it was a caribou. They had been out hunting. That was why they weren't waiting for him.

Uncle James pulled another carcass up, then pushed it over the grassy, sloping bank. As it slid down, James held onto the antlers and dug them into the ground, to break the caribou's momentum.

"Hi, Daddy! Hi, Uncle James!" Paul called out, excitedly.

Both men nodded and James said: "Grab hold here, Paul."

Paul halted his excited rush with a couple of faltering steps, grabbed an antler branch in each hand and started tugging. He quickly dropped his wide grin and, embarrassment at his childish enthusiasm burning within, he silently fell to work with the men.

The caribou were finally rolled over into the skiff, and Paul took his usual place forward, as James pushed off. The motor cranked to a high whine and the boat headed out into the whitecaps.

After watching the waves roll beneath the boat for a couple of minutes, Paul stole a backward glance at the men. Paul's dad now looked at him and broke into a tight grin. Paul weakly smiled back. He glanced over at James, who was already staring at him, as if he had been watching Paul for some time now. James had a habit of sometimes looking at Paul that way: as if he were trying to see something inside Paul, or just look past him—Paul couldn't ever decide which. James wasn't much of a talker, but sometimes Paul had the feeling that James was trying to talk to him—yet not in words. It was confusing. James didn't smile, just looked at Paul with those piercing eyes of his, as they now met Paul's, then looked away to watch the waves. Paul felt uncomfortable and turned around to watch the waves, too, just in time to get some spray in his face.

The caribou turned out to be Christmas dinner. Money was getting a little tight in the village, so hunted food became more important, with cash going only on staples. The caribou this time of year were pretty lean, but at least they were available. So, when James and Dick spotted the small herd across the bay, close to where Paul was to show up, they set out immediately, hurriedly loading the boat and barely beaching it when they landed.

The meat wasn't the most tender by any means, since it had only hung overnight, yet it was still nourishing, and the flavor brought back a flood of satisfying memories to all who partook of it—and that meant the entire village. Even when the village had been larger, sharing food and visiting from house to house was a tradition for holidays. Now, with only five families living in Ichinski, they all managed to squeeze into the former school building and have their Christmas dinner together.

It was utter confusion, of course, with the children underfoot and meal preparations going on, but everyone loved it that way. The women good-naturedly argued about what food was ready and where it should be placed while, gathered in a group, the men laughed and ribbed each other about remembered hunting disasters, or the latest incidents in Biorka. While the youngest children played and fussed under tables and chairs, the older ones tracked snow into the house as they yelled a request, only to be shooed outside to play some more.

Paul loved it all! It had always been the one time he could depend on for daily privations and family squabbles to be set aside, and for unity and comradeship to reign in the village again.

By the time it was late afternoon, Paul was so full of caribou roast, carrots, potatoes, pie, cake and rolls that he could hardly move. He sat contentedly on some pillows, leaning up against a wall. Other kids were similarly satiated and resting.

Most of the adults were talking and seated around the big table, which was thrown together out of four doors and some sawhorses. A few others, including the older folks, slumped on the sofa or slept in chairs. Grandma Surikov was snoring loudly, her head thrown back against the top of the sofa. Children were curled up everywhere.

Paul settled back into his comfortable corner, content with the peaceful scene about him. The heat of the wood stove made him sleepy, and he relished its soothing effect. The stove sent out flickers of flames dancing in the dimmed room, and the smell of burning alder accented the air. The thought slowly turned over and over in his mind: If only it could be like this forever... If only it could be... He dozed off.

It seemed to Paul as though he had been sleeping for years, floating in a warm sea which gently rocked him, when he woke up to laughter and music. Uncle James and Eddy Dirks were tuning their guitars, Grandma had her concertina out and Franklin Miller was scratching around on an old, beat-up fiddle. After some attempts at tuning them all, they reached an approximation and the music began. At first, the players were a little stiff in technique and mannerisms, but in no time at all they livened up, considerably.

Grandma was sitting on a stool with a big grin on her face, fairly making the stool jump about, as if it were her dancing partner. James and Eddy kept competing in flourishes of technique, ignoring the mistakes and giving each other a grin and a laugh when things got too mixed up.

Uncle James was quite a guitar player, and Paul had heard him play popular tunes like those on the stereo tapes, as well as lots of old Russian Aleut songs, and something James called "Country and Blues". Franklin was all over the place, hamming it up to the extreme—nearly coming to tears with the sad songs, and leaping from chair to chair like a clown with the sillier ones. Paul and the rest of the audience loved it.

It was a good show, and went on for a couple of hours, with pauses for refreshment, which added to the liveliness of the group. Slowly, though, families said their goodbyes and went on back home, mocking seriousness and knowing full well they would see each other in a little while when the starring began.

And, of course, around eight o'clock Paul could hear people laughing and singing, moving through the village. By this time, Paul and his family were home, and he rushed to the window to look outside. The sight which greeted him lifted him back to the fading world of a small child's Christmas excitement.

Outlined on a large, wooden wheel-frame, four feet across, was a wooden star, with its points divided into sets of three. Decorating the star's many sections were strings of shiny tinsel, which glittered in the light of the kerosene lamps. The person holding the handle at the wheel's axle kept the star turning, as the group of people moved from house to house. At each door, a jovial demand for refreshments was made, and the group invited inside to sing and have a drink. After their request was met, the star was again taken up and, singing, the group moved on. Starring was always something to look forward to at Christmas, and it ended what was usually a very happy day.

After a couple more stops, the entire village was now with the starring group, and only the Surikov house was left. Shouting and banging on the door they arrived, and Grandma helped James and Dick set out glasses for the traditional drink of liquor. The adults were already well lubricated, and the children were getting wild, so it made quite a disordered affair.

Someone started an old Russian folk song, and everyone broke out in a raucous voice. As this was the last stop, most of the adults squeezed into the house and settled into singing and conversation—with some more Christmas cheer. Mrs. Dirks took the youngest children and went home to put them to bed, while the other adults all stayed.

During the day, there hadn't been much drinking but, now that the day was over, the lid was to come off. Paul knew things could get rough during the night, with arguments and all, so he took some blankets and crawled into his customary "safe spot", under one of the low shelves in the storage room. It wasn't too cold there and, besides, it was a lot better than getting woken up in the middle of the night. He had hidden like this many times before, so it wasn't anything much for him to think about, as he drifted off to sleep, still thinking of the happy times of the day.

Paul spent the rest of his vacation playing with the village children, or wandering alone over his favorite haunts: at the rocks on the point, along the beach or back on the hillside, under a thicket of secluded alders. The thought of Biorka and the life he led there hardly crossed his mind for the first few days, but, once Christmas was over, memories of that life flared up increasingly. Reality now slowly crept back into the forefront of his awareness, like a persistent cat, hungry for a plate of milk, but wary of the stranger offering it.

One blustery day, Paul took a longer hike with his cousins, Willie and Mary. Even though the wind that day was blowing the snow fiercely, it wasn't too cold if they kept moving, and they found shelter shortly. Their destination was a hideout: a small rock shelter in a ravine, to which they had added driftwood walls over the years. The wind whistled ominously overhead, and snow drifted deep around the shelter's side. But the doorway remained free, from which the children could watch the sea, as gusts of wind flattened the waves into a sheet of spray, before passing on.

Paul and his cousins had arrived late in the morning, started a fire and ate a lunch of dried salmon, tea and pilot bread. They snuggled together, up against a wood backrest of boards which faced the fire. It was very cozy. *Too* cozy, since Willie fell asleep and Paul was inclined to do likewise.

However, as he sat staring at the flickering dance of

flames, his thoughts drifted back to his new life in Biorka. Before vacation, he wanted nothing more than to escape that place. All those thoughts were painful memories of loneliness, confusion and intimidation; he remembered Ichinski as a miniature Heaven. But, now that he had returned, and satisfied his cravings for security and familiarity with people and places of his past, the distinction was no longer so clearly defined. Instead of the painful memories of Biorka, his musings now brought up some pleasant images of events to go to, such as the basketball games and occasional movies—and even of the school itself.

He had some friends now, too, and it was these that he pictured the most when Biorka came to mind. One boy in particular, Moses Yatchmenof, was his best friend. Moses never made fun of Paul's clothes, or how he spoke or acted; Moses seemed to understand all of this. After all, he was also from a village—Atka—and he too had once had to make the adjustments Paul was undergoing.

Yet, beyond this common background, Moses seemed to have a special peace within himself—a calmness that allowed him to take everything in stride and not become upset. Paul, in contrast, tended to react immediately to everything. He was very defensive, and this fed the taunting by the Biorka children. Paul was genuinely mystified at this difference, and once asked Moses about it: how he could take the ugly things kids said to him. Moses looked at him for a moment, then said simply: "We Aleuts must be strong within ourselves. My grandfather told me that, and I believe him."

Paul asked Moses what he meant by "within ourselves",

but Moses couldn't explain it any more than that his grandfather had said it is to know who you are, and to be proud of it. That made sense to Paul—he was Aleut and proud of it—but somehow it didn't fully answer his question.

In Paul's mind, the people at Biorka called themselves Aleut and seemed to be proud of that, but they didn't much look or act like Aleuts. They hardly knew any Aleut words, nor how to hunt and fish in the old ways. They spent lots of money on snowmobiles and motorcycles and refrigerators and washing machines and lots of other things, and if they broke down, the people just left them out in the weather to rust, when they couldn't get parts sent out to fix them. This all confused Paul, because none of this way of living was what he learned from his grandfather and dad about how the Aleut way should be: a proud and resourceful way.

So, when Moses told Paul his understanding of his grandfather's message, Paul was confused even more. Which is the Aleut way? What is an Aleut then, anyway, when you start thinking about it? These questions rolled through Paul's mind, like the waves of the sea—except that these waves had yet to find a solid shore upon which to break.

The fire was crackling and still well-fueled. Paul looked through the partially blocked doorway, at the drifting snow and back down to the fire, taking great pleasure in the warmth it radiated. Sitting next to him, Mary shifted her position and settled down again.

Without turning, Paul whispered: "Mary?"

"Yeah?" she softly answered.

"You want to go back?"

Mary was silent, thinking about the shift to Biorka for schooling that she and Willie had also experienced. She hesitated. "I don't know." She turned to look at Paul; "You thinking about it, too?"

"Yeah," Paul replied, then was silent. He then began again: "I really wanted to get out of that place and get back here. Coming back was okay, too, for a while. Now that we gotta go back in a couple of days, though, I'm kinda mixed up. I mean, it's good to be here and do all the stuff we used to do, but... well, it's different somehow." He paused, digging the dirt with a stick. With a sudden sigh of exasperation, he tossed the small stick in the fire and leaned back.

Mary sat looking at him, her large, brown eyes staring from the recesses of her parka, where a forelock of long, brown hair straggled down one side. She would be a rather attractive woman someday, given a little instruction in the art of beauty care. But, for now, she was just a rather skinny, awkward young girl.

After Paul's words, her face brightened somewhat. "Me too. Holy, all I wanted to do was get here. But, now I'm here, it ain't like it used to be; something's changed. There's stuff I miss in Biorka: the movies, TV, friends to play with, stuff we do in school... We ain't got that here, and I miss it all now."

Both children remained silent. Mary finally spoke up again: "Willie's glad to be home, though. He sure misses Mom and Dad; he still cries a lot at night. I heard them talking that maybe they'd keep Willie here for the rest of the year." She paused. "I guess he's too young to go out there like us."

They both looked over at Willie, bundled up in his parka,

big boots and snow pants, sleeping soundly with his head propped against a log. Paul thought, with envy: *Too little to be bothered; too little to even know the difference! People just take care of him. With me, there's no choice, I guess.*

Willie stirred and looked around. "What you guys been doing?"

"Just talkin'," Mary replied.

"About what?"

"Just stuff you wouldn't care about: big kid stuff."

Satisfied with the explanation, Willie began to rustle about and complain of being hungry.

Paul stood to peer out through the doorway, at the sky. Even though the wind was still howling, and snow was scooting in a sheet over the ground, the sky was fairly clear and the sun shone dimly through a haze of overcast. It was early afternoon, but already it was getting darker.

"We better go," Paul announced to the others, and they all bundled up, tightly. Paul dumped snow on the fire embers and got Willie and Mary outside. He hesitated and glanced around at the shelter, in a habitual check for any loose boards or logs. *It's nice to have a cozy place like this, alright,* he thought.

As always when he came here, Paul felt a twinge of regret at having to leave, but this time there was something more: he had this clutching feeling for a moment that, just maybe, he wouldn't see the hideout again, for a very long time—maybe never. Such a thought had never occurred before, since everything had always been a certainty. Now? Well, he just didn't know. Suddenly, the place felt strange to him, as if he had never been there before.

"Paul!" Mary stuck her head back in the entrance. "Come on, we're freezin' out here!"

"Okay." Paul went out, pulled a big plank across the opening, and set out toward home with the other children.

13
Shake-Up

Cal

After vacation, life in Biorka settled into the old daily rhythm and routine. The crab plant was going strong, processing tanners with a good catch and a steady supply. At least one sixty- to one-hundred-foot boat docked every day or so. The beach was covered with a perpetual frosting of whitish-tan crushed crab shells, dumped from the cannery.

Not too much was done about the burnt cannery buildings, except to begin the slow process of debris removal, whenever the weather permitted. After some delay, they finally decided to rebuild. However, it would take at least a year and a half to complete the new facility. In the meantime, next season's catch would be processed at Arctic Queen's Nagal Pass facility, closed down five years previously because of poor salmon runs then. At least, those were the present plans; no one ever took any such talk too seriously. After all, big plans like these could be—and, in the past, had been—changed completely, without the locals hearing anything about it until the consequences of the change occurred.

Stores in town were restocked by two small freighters,

which brought in some badly needed items. For a couple of days, families splurged on the luxury of perishable items, then it was back to staples again.

The diesel generating plant broke down twice, and the town was without electricity for ten hours the first time and two days the second. Frozen and refrigerated foods were stacked out on the open back porches of houses, to keep them from spoiling. Such outages were common in Biorka and happened at least three times a month, but usually only for a half-hour.

School started again, and the children resignedly went through their paces. Since it was difficult for them to see any relevance of what they learned in class to their tightly knit world of Biorka, few were enthused about their work, and most did just enough to get by. After all, what need did a fisherman have of facts about the social upheaval of post-World War One Germany, or the basics of algebraic computation? And, why was it important for a future housewife to understand the poetry of Robert Frost, or to be able to identify the internal organs of a dissected frog? What relevance did these have to their futures—at least, to their expected futures? True or not, that is what their limited experience with the outside world led them to think.

Besides these problems, Cal also suffered from another difficulty with his studies. He had been so involved in playing basketball and acting the hero role that he had almost completely neglected doing any classwork at all. And what Coach Irving said to him, one practice after school, didn't aid in his ability to concentrate. Irving casually remarked to Cal that he should think about trying to get a scholarship, to play at a college somewhere in Alaska.

The remark had caught him off-guard and, since it was simply mentioned then dropped, Cal didn't know what to say back. He just kind of stood there, flat-footed and said: "Oh."

Yet, regardless of its brevity, the suggestion did prick his interest. All that day it kept popping up in his mind, turned over and over like a strange but beautiful stone.

Cal never thought much about where basketball would take him; it was just something you did in school if you were good enough. After graduating from school, you got together for a few games with the town team, to play other teams on the Peninsula and Islands, and that was it. Now the coach had tied this restricted concept of the game to the outside world, and it was this mental struggle of trying to figure out the implications of this tie that disturbed Cal's sleep that night.

The next day, during practice, Cal found a chance to ask more. The coach was alone on the sidelines, drawing out some plays, when Cal, taking advantage of chasing a loose ball, stopped and quickly asked: "Hey, uh, Coach?"

"Yes?" Irving quietly replied as he finished a drawing.

"Uh, what was that you said about playing at a college or something?" Cal hated to ask, but his curiosity was too great.

The coach looked puzzled for a second or two, then feigned enlightenment. "Oh, yes! You mean playing for a college ball team."

Cal nodded in agreement.

"Well, what I was wondering was what you'll be doing after you graduate. I've never heard you say anything, so I thought I'd mention the possibility of your going to college and perhaps getting a basketball scholarship." Irving watched Cal's face closely for any expressions, but none emerged. He continued: "I think you do well enough to play in a small college and get some expenses paid for playing. You probably could get a scholarship to one of the small colleges in Sitka or Anchorage, or maybe to the U-of-A in Fairbanks or Anchorage. It would give you a chance to get some additional schooling and play some ball at the same time." The coach looked intently at Cal.

Nothing, not a twitch.

Cal looked down and pushed some imaginary dirt on the floor, with his right foot. "Takes a lot of money to do that," Cal finally said, and looked up at Irving.

"Yes, it takes a fair amount, but you shouldn't have to pay too much, because the Aleut Corporation could take care of a lot of the costs, since you're Aleut. And I assume you've got some savings from fishing?" He paused while Cal shifted his weight to the other foot and looked around.

Irving could see Cal was getting nervous about this, so he cut it short. "You think about it, and if you want to find out more, let me know. I can help you write for applications and things like that. Okay?"

Cal nodded, bounced the ball twice and turned to rejoin the team. Irving watched Cal as he went back to shooting practice. In a few moments, Irving too turned back to work.

Cal didn't have it all straight in his head yet, and

consequently tried to forget the conversation... but he couldn't.

Another thing which troubled him was Catherine: she didn't seem to be her usual self anymore. She was quiet and even sullen at times—not at all cheerful, like she customarily was. Sometimes, when she walked by Cal in the hallway, she didn't even glance at him. It wasn't the same coy trick she often played when she was with other girls, laughing with them and purposefully ignoring him to flirt; no, she was often by herself and deeply absorbed in thought. At other times, she would suddenly take notice of him when she looked up, and sheepishly smile.

It was all rather confusing to Cal, but didn't deeply disturb him; he was used to passing off such an inability to understand female behavior as "women", as his father used the term. Besides, he was too caught up in doing stuff with the guys and with basketball to allow himself to think about Catherine's change very much.

So, his twinge of curiosity and concern faded, and he wrapped himself in his own very personal interests.

14
Shake-Up

Catherine

Truly, as Cal noticed, Catherine *had* changed. What started as a pin-prick in Mrs. Irving's class had grown into a painful ache. Now, somehow, she couldn't shake the question, "What are the choices you have in Biorka?" or Ruth's crazy scheme of them going to college together.

Catherine would be in class, concentrating on Mr. Campbell's explanation of a point in shorthand technique, then, before she realized it, her thoughts would have drifted off completely, to daydreaming about herself attending college classes or working at a big-city job. Several times teachers had caught her inattentiveness, and she had to ask to have their questions repeated. It was uncomfortable to have this happen, but Catherine couldn't seem to shake it. She couldn't get those thoughts out of her head.

During vacation, she worked at the crab-can building, a few days when one of the regulars couldn't make it. She was glad to get the money, but what she thought of and saw there made her even more confused.

She worked with nine other women, several of them young and recently married. They stood at the packing table, taking crab meat out of the big trays, packing it in the small cans, weighing each can for the correct amount and putting them on the conveyor belt, which went to the sealing machine. The women all wore large, white aprons and caps, rubber gloves and boots, and gaily chatted with each other about this and that: the gossip of the town, how their children were doing, or what their husbands were working on. Meanwhile, the machinery hummed and clanked, and the lights burnt brightly in the working area, fading into the recesses of the building. On and on this went, hour after hour. After work, the women pulled their hooded coats close against the chilly wind, and went home to their domestic duties.

Catherine watched these women for hours on end and wondered about them, about herself and her future. She wondered… and got nowhere.

Back in school, it was no better: she watched her friends and saw in them the white-aproned, rubber-protected women of the cannery—the mothers-to-be, who would raise more girls, to in turn become white-aproned, rubber-protected women… That was as far as she could get.

That life was the known, but she wasn't sure she liked it. She was tempted by the unknown, the Outside, yet she feared it, too. She felt caught and she hated it.

15
Storm

It was in the latter part of January that the storm came.

The Aleutian Islands chain is called the "Cradle of Storms", and for good reason. It and the Alaska Peninsula form a barrier between the warm Kuro Shio Current, moving up the south side from Japan, and the cold Bering Sea currents circulating on the north side, between Siberia and Southwest Alaska. The meeting of cold and warm air above these sea currents and the Asian air masses moving over from Siberia leads to huge atmospheric disturbances. These become major Alaskan storm centers, eventually influencing the weather down the west coast of North America and further inland as well. Sometimes, conditions are such that a formidable storm lasts for weeks, and this January was the start of one of those storms.

On the day of its beginning, Paul was on his way to school in the early morning darkness, along with the other children. As was his habit each morning, checking the day's weather, he peered through the dark at the distant sea horizon, and tested the quality of the air in his nose and on his lips.

He sniffed deeply. It hadn't rained or snowed for a week, though heavy clouds had rolled overhead continuously. In truth, it had felt very dry. This morning, however, the air was heavy with moisture—so heavy it seemed to press down tight upon every living thing above the ground.

The temperature was below freezing, and everyone's breath condensed in a fog about them. So, the boardwalk now carried a small cloud above it, as the students went by. Only a couple of other children noticed the strange weather that morning, since most were hurrying to get to school and their friends. To Paul, though, it was an invigorating experience to sense the phenomenon, and he stepped off to the side to take it in. He listened for any bird sounds, normally starting now, but there were none. Paul waited a few moments more, to give the dense air time to register in his memory, then stepped back to the boardwalk and hurried to school.

Paul had been right in his guesses about the weather signs. He and Moses excitedly sought each other out and shared impressions of their clues to the coming storm. When the noon break came, the two rushed outdoors and spent the half-hour watching the gulls and other shorebirds, nervously flying out against the rising wind, seeking protection in the lee of the cannery wharf pilings. The boys stood sheltered beside the wall of the school building, talking about past storms and watching the birds. Just as the bell rang, and they went inside, the first snowflakes began falling.

Throughout the afternoon, the snow fell in a continuous, swirling mass, as it blew into whirlwinds behind buildings and flattened into driving sheets over bare ground. Immediately, snowdrifts built rapidly. The temperature dropped to only around 20°F but, with a 25 mph wind, the cold pierced one's clothing like a thousand tiny needles. By two o'clock, conditions had become so severe that school was dismissed early, for fear of elementary children getting lost going home in the driving snow.

With cheers, the older students burst through the doors and into the blast of cold and stinging snow. The small school bus loaded a group of younger children and set off, returning shortly for another load. Within the half-hour, all students were home and settled in, waiting until the storm stopped and they could play outside.

However, the wait was in vain; the next day was worse. Households twenty feet apart could barely see each other. The wind was gusting to 35 mph and drifts blocked the entrance to nearly every home. Word went out on the phone lines that school was canceled for the next two days, and the crab cannery closed down as well.

For those two days, no one stirred outside, except for emergencies, of which luckily there were few. The water pipes in most houses froze, and many oil and propane lines did, too, somehow having gotten water in the line or regulator. Fortunately, the town's electrical generator kept humming and, taking advantage of this blessing, people could often be seen scurrying from house to house, carrying an electric heater to share with a family whose fuel lines had frozen.

Perhaps best off were those few houses which still depended on wood for heat and cooking. Families living in these houses spent the time comfortably in the kitchen, enjoying the warmth put out by the big old cooking stoves.

Moses's family was one of these. On Atka, they mainly used driftwood and scrub alders for fuel; having limited expensive fuel oil available, this was their customary way of cooking and heating. Moses's family was extremely poor by Biorka standards, but when the wind blew, the snow drifted deep and other more modern means of heating and cooking failed, the Yatchmenofs chuckled inwardly, as they remembered how others had chided them for their backward ways.

Now, as they sat cheerily in the kitchen, sharing their comfort with a few close neighbors, who were driven from their homes by the cold, father Yatchmenof was extremely gracious and benevolent in sharing their meager facilities and food—and enjoyed the chance to better his detractors.

"Yes," he would solemnly say, "the old Aleut ways are no good anymore. We must somehow save and get one of those new stoves one day." With a twinkle in his eye, he would flash a smile at Moses and their guests.

On Sunday, four days after the storm began, it let up enough that people could dig themselves out and get to the stores, which had announced they would be open that afternoon. Although the wind was still around 15 mph, most of the snow in the air was kicked up off the ground by the wind, and was not newly fallen. Indeed, most of the snow during the entire storm was not new, but simply moved from place to place.

Outside their houses, the residents found a vastly changed landscape. Instead of the usual flat ground on which the town was sited, they found a variegated scene of white shapes and brown patches of bare ground. The eaves of each house sloped from the roof to the ground in a continuous bank of drifted snow. On the lee side of the drift, a sharp edge was formed, as if scooped out by a giant ice-cream dipper. Every building had a similar drift and, behind every obstacle—rock, oil drum, smoke shed or clump of grass—was a drift smoothed to leeward, and cut sharp on the knife-like ridge.

Getting out of the house was the first task people faced; then, after that, it was tunneling through the drifts which blocked the way between houses. Almost as bad was the drifting snow, which stealthily sneaked back to slowly fill up the efforts of moments ago. However, the townspeople got outside and a few older children, bundled up tightly in snowsuits and boots, stumbled out to roll and plow through the drifts near their houses.

As afternoon darkness encroached, everyone headed back home—after having replenished food supplies, thawed pipes and started bulky heaters—and settled in for the night, to see what the next day might hold.

School opened for a few days, but then closed again as the storm renewed. People stayed inside.

When the wind and snow abated somewhat, they dug out, stocked up on necessities and made repairs. The storm would close in again, the school would shut down and everyone would stay home.

And so it went for three weeks, before the wind and snow finally stopped, and the sun shone bright and clear.

Then it was the old magic again. Silence reigned and people wandered about outside, just enjoying the escape from confinement, and the continual stress of the banging and pounding of the wind. The warmth of the radiant sun on their faces was an added gift, which made it a genuine pleasure to enjoy the blissful peace. It only lasted for a couple of days, as usual, but in that short period people could get ready to face the next onslaught, and the inevitable news of tragedies.

During the clear weather, the Goose flew several flights a day, ferrying mail and passengers to and from Biorka. With this source of contact came news and gossip of the Islands chain and the Peninsula.

A large crab boat had been caught off Chignik by the storm and sank with all hands on board. One of the wheeled RAA planes crashed on a medical emergency to the village of Nelson Lagoon. It had landed safely but, during takeoff, it was blown back to the ground by an extremely strong gust of wind, and crashed off the end of the gravel runway, out on the frozen hummocked tundra. The passenger in the plane—who had already burnt her hand and face badly in an oil stove flare-up—had to wait four more days for another plane. By then, her damage was extremely severe, and they flew her on to Seattle for specialty care.

At the same time, more personal disasters were developing for those at Biorka.

Paul's uncle Damien and family, who lived at an isolated spot on Umnat Island, ran out of food and made a dash in their skiff to Nicolski, twenty-five miles distant, where supplies were available. The entire family of seven had set out together, since there was no telling when they could get back home. Their skiff never reached its destination. Several days later, a party of hunters stopped at the remote homestead and found the house vacated and bare of food. When the hunters mentioned this at the store in Nicolski, the storekeeper figured that the Andreanofs had set out to replenish their supplies, as they had done many times before, but somehow had not made it. The State Troopers were alerted, along with the Coast Guard, but the newly returned foul weather prevented a search. Julian Golodoff heard the news at the cannery office, when it came in over the radio-telephone, and told Paul, knowing the Andreanofs were relatives.

"They're probably blown off on a beach someplace," Julian commented off-handedly, trying to keep fears down. "It happens all the time."

Paul knew that was true. It had even happened to him and his dad once, and it wasn't a pleasant thing to live through. It had been four days before they were pulled off of that rainy, windswept, barren islet. Now here was Uncle Damien and Auntie Vi with the rest of the family, out in some similar situation—except they had the biting cold and snow to fight, instead of rain. Paul's stomach rolled uneasily when he thought about them, conjuring up the unpleasantness of his own experience. As he looked out of the window, at the drifting snow and windswept waves in the bay, Paul found it difficult to fight down the growing certainty he felt of the family's fate.

During the lull, Cal also had cause for worry. While his family was busy with repairs and other chores, Cal's uncle, Walter Larsen, flew out on the first plane to Sand Point. Since salmon runs had been so good the last couple of years, Walter decided to sell his small gill-netter and purchase a sixty-foot purse-seiner. The boat was in Kodiak and, with the papers signed, all that remained was to bring it to Biorka.

The boat had a powerful diesel engine and could turn a steady twelve knots cruising, so the trip wouldn't take but about two days at most, running continuously—if the good weather and calm seas continued.

Walter's twenty-five-year-old son, Bob, and a friend of his went along for the ride, and to help in case of an emergency. Within six hours after leaving Kodiak, they radioed that they were on their way, having set out into the night with fairly calm seas and a star-studded sky.

By the morning of the second day of clear weather in Biorka, the temperature rose slightly and high, flat clouds began sheeting the skies. In the late afternoon the wind picked up, and by night it was howling loudly, as it drove newly fallen snow before it. As the snow swept over drifts and around buildings, and darkness enveloped the town, families settled in peacefully to face the new onslaught.

That is, most of them did. Walter Larsen's family and Cal's family had hoped Walter would get the new boat in before the storm broke, but it didn't happen. Now, the family members had to face the unexpected with optimism they knew was not justified.

Back in school a few days later, Catherine was in the hall, talking with Ruth and Alice during a class break, when she noticed Mr. Parkhurst motion for Cal to come with him to the office.

Normally, Cal would make a pretense of resistance to being called in to see the principal—an act which always got some chuckles from bystanders. This time, however, Cal simply left his locker and walked right along with Parkhurst. It must be about Walter, Catherine thought.

The bell rang and she went on to class, knowing that Cal would be in soon, and she could find out then what had happened—if that was what it was about. Half the period went by, though, and still no Cal.

As was her habit about this time of day, she got up to go outside for a drink, from the fountain around the corner. Absent-mindedly, she made the turn and pulled up short, surprised. There, leaning against the wall, was Cal.

He was upset and had obviously cried but was now trying to pull himself together. They were both taken aback by the unexpected encounter, and for a couple of seconds stared dumbly at each other.

Catherine spoke first: "Cal, what happened? Was it about Walter?"

Cal turned slightly away, embarrassed at being seen before

he had collected himself, yet relieved to have someone to share his distress.

"Yeah," he finally answered, "Walter's boat was swamped and sunk, somewhere off Unga Island. Walter is okay, and so is Pat… but Bob drowned."

As he said the last words, his voice trembled and he choked slightly, tears welling in his eyes. Cal's cousin had been like a big brother to him, their having played together since childhood, and was an exemplary and promising young fisherman, which made Cal all the more admiring of him.

Catherine suddenly felt a strong desire to reach out and comfort Cal, but she couldn't. This was school, and hidden eyes were everywhere. Besides, she wasn't sure enough of Cal anymore to know whether he would accept or reject her offer. She stood as though rooted to the floor, tense and searching Cal's face for any signs of understanding her conflict.

Tradition and uncertainty likewise tied Cal, and he could only stand there, torn by newfound emotions of desire for surrender and comfort, yet cautious of how such an outward demonstration would be accepted by Catherine, by prying eyes… by himself.

The welling of feeling between the two peaked and, as if by common signal, waned. It was gone… the magic moment, the opportunity.

Cal felt drained. He stood up straight, rubbed his eyes and faked a yawn. "Well," he stated, "I'd better get to class."

"Are you okay now?" Catherine gently asked, seeking yet some small measure of sharing between them.

Cal looked at her, almost tenderly, and smiled: "Yeah."

The smile broadened, then fell slightly. "Thanks, Cath."

He reached out and took her hand for a moment, then turned and went to class. A few moments later, Catherine followed.

After school the following day, Mary told Paul when he got home that the Andreanof family had finally been located. Everyone had made it except Grandma: she died after three days. As presumed, the storm had driven them ashore, onto a barren, rocky beach, where their boat had overturned and broken up. All the meager supplies they had taken along were lost, except for the rifle—little Paul had saved that.

Luckily, the rifle was loaded, so they had six shells to use. Two were used to start a small fire, which was thereafter kept going continually by all members, scavenging for dry fuel. They used the remaining four shells to shoot two foxes and a small seal, which got away, only to be found washed ashore the next day. Other than the meat, the family survived on frozen tundra berries, sea urchins and shellfish.

The food wasn't so much a problem as was protection from the storm. The small island they landed on was almost featureless, except for a small, rocky bluff on the windward side. Since it was too windy and exposed near the bluff, they searched until they found shelter in a four-foot-deep ravine, which they roofed over with driftwood. In this small enclosure, they managed to hang on for two weeks, until a passing fishing boat was attracted by their waving, ragged forms and the smoke from their smoldering fire.

Asked where they wanted to go, they continued to their original destination of the store at Nicolski, charged for their food supplies—plus some clothing now needing replacement—and headed back to their home via another fishing boat, which was going in that direction. In their minds, there was no question of where to go; it was just a matter of finishing their original journey.

Before setting off, they wrote to a brother, in hopes that he could drop another skiff by their home. Until that happened, they would have to wait, and continue their traditional occupation of basic survival.

16
Visit

Paul

A few weeks into February the storm finally broke. Late one night, the wind shifted abruptly to the south and blew very hard. Houses creaked with the first gusts of the new menace, and radio lines strung along the rooftops hummed. Everyone listened intently to the roar, but this time there was something different that gave them hope.

With the wind came warm air, and on this warm air rode dense sheets of rain, which began to slowly wear at the icy ridges of the tall drifts, and the packed snow and ice which stood a foot deep over everything. The long storm was over and spring was on its way—not immediately coming, as if it ever appeared suddenly in this monotone climate, but at least on its way. Almost breathing an audible sigh of relief, the town settled in for a night's rest, thinking with anticipation of the morrow and the days ahead.

The rain steadily wore away at the snowy sheath and, after four days, only the largest drifts and thickest ice remained. The ice on the lagoon broke up on the fifth day, and, on an afternoon's ebbing tide, most of the six-inch-thick ice floated out. Since the lagoon entrance was not extremely wide, ice jam after ice jam formed and broke, leaving large piles of broken ice sheets shoved high on the shore. The ice chunks in the bay made small boat navigation dangerous, but this too only lasted a couple of days. Soon, the bay was again free, and it was a week later that Paul's dad and uncle made it through and visited him.

Dick and James had been over to Biorka on several trips, since Paul had arrived there for school in September. Usually, though, Paul never saw them, since they just came for mail and supplies, and to visit the bar. They didn't bother to check on Paul and see how he was doing—instead, they took off again as soon as they got what they wanted. The first time they came and left, Paul was deeply hurt that they didn't see him but, after a night of restless sleep, the ache seemed to go away, and Paul took it as just his dad's way.

The two times Paul did see them, though, both men had been drinking. Paul hadn't realized this on the first occasion, when he saw them from a distance, as they were loading up the skiff. He had run forward toward them, shouting: "Daddy! Uncle James!" It was only when he was almost to them, when his dad looked up, grinned and waved, that Paul comprehended their condition. James just sat in the boat.

"Hi, boy," Dick greeted. "How ya been doin', huh? You been good now, ain'tcha?" He said it in mock seriousness, then broke into his lopsided, drunken grin again. He slapped the boy hard on the shoulder and fell heavily against him for support.

"Yeah, I've been okay," Paul answered, straight-faced.

"You been studyin'? You learnin' lotsa stuff, right?"

"Yeah, I'm learnin'."

"Well, you keep up the good work, now." Dick paused and looked around, distracted for a moment, then turned to Paul again, though not looking at him. "We gotta go now, get this stuff home." He paused again, thinking. "You got money… to buy stuff?" He looked at Paul.

Paul shrugged his shoulders.

"Well, I had lots w'me, but I hadda buy lots'a stuff t'day." Dick pointed a wavering finger at the boat: inside was a pile of food boxes and cases of beer. "Got no more left!" He grinned widely and pulled both pockets inside-out, to show that they were empty.

He then laughed loudly, gave Paul another swat on the back and tousled his hair, roughly. "Gotta go now," he announced, as he unsteadily started to shove the skiff into the water. Paul helped push, since the two weren't doing very well, and off they went.

Paul watched for a couple of moments, then turned up the beach, his head hung down. The rest of that day was hard for Paul to get through.

The next time Paul ran into his father when he had been drinking, Paul got away as quickly as he could.

This time, he also noticed how some of the townspeople passing by reacted to his dad and uncle: they said nothing right then, but he could tell by the way they turned their heads and laughed loudly, after walking farther on, that they were scornful of the men. Paul overheard some of their cutting remarks, too. Biorka residents sometimes talked like that about their own excessive drinkers, but with outside villagers, the words had a particular venom in the way they were said. For the first time in his life, it embarrassed Paul to be seen with his father and uncle. He had always felt disgusted by their stupid and often crude actions when drunk—he felt the same way about all adults who got drunk—but he had never felt the burning shame that now came in the presence of strangers.

It didn't help, either, when he would overhear Julian and Mary talking about his family, or others from Ichinski. Julian would talk about what a fool Paul's dad had made of himself during the last visit to town, when he and James had to haul Dick outside the bar to keep him from fighting with somebody. And kids at school would tease Paul about his dad falling down drunk on the boardwalk, and sleeping there for part of the night, before he was found, half-frozen, and taken to the nurse, to thaw out and sober up.

At first Paul got mad and argued, but it didn't do any good; there were too many against him. So, after a while, he learned to turn a deaf ear and walk away, as best he could. At any rate, by the time his father and uncle purposely came to the Golodoffs' to see him, Paul was sufficiently hardened to the matter of public opinion, so the event wasn't completely devastating.

At school that rainy day, Moses mentioned to Paul that his dad and uncle, and Fred Dirks as well, had come to town last evening. They had stopped by Moses's house for an hour, before going on to the cannery bunkhouse, where some buddies had let them in to stay the night. He said they were still quite sober, but they had a lot of money which they said they were going to spend on supplies. Evidently, all of them had gotten the last salmon settlement check from the cannery.

All that day, Paul was torn between a genuine desire to have the familiarity of the men's companionship and his apprehension about the strong likelihood of running into them half-drunk again. He was also more than mildly curious about the rumor of money.

Whenever Biorka or Ichinski men had just received a big check and started drinking, they were usually generous in giving money to kids; they liked to make a big show of loading their kids up with cash, or taking them to the store to buy a coat, some boots or several big boxes of candy and gum. It was like a little Christmas. Truthfully, it was always better to get gifts instead of money, because when the men sobered up they would want their money back. With the food or clothing, you could spend the night tucked away in a secret place, eating candy bars and wearing the clothing, to make it used and non-returnable.

The opportunity for such an occasion wasn't all that frequent, but it was always exciting to dream and hope. So, with a mixture of dread and hope, Paul slowly made his way home after school.

When he arrived, everything was normal. At dinner, nothing was said or seemed unusual, so Paul began to relax, as his suspicion diminished. About eight o'clock there was a knock at the door, but Paul hardly noticed.

Julian answered and, as the voices of the guests rose higher in greeting, Paul's heart skipped a beat. Into the living room came his dad, Uncle James, Fred Dirks and another man whom Paul didn't know. Instinctively, Paul stood up and timidly grinned. "Hi, Daddy," he said.

"Hi, Paul," his dad said effusively, as he strode across the room to put an arm around his son's shoulder. "You look pretty good," he stated. Turning to Julian and his wife, he said with a broad grin: "You must feed him a lot." They all laughed together, and Dick walked over to join the rest of the adults at the kitchen table.

Well, at least he hasn't been drinking, Paul realized. He was safe for now, and his attention turned to visions of money and gifts.

His mind rambled over such images as he sat in the living room, half playing with a model airplane and half listening to the talk at the table. Julian brought out some beer for these village men, with whom he shared a common background, and the conversation continued.

Shortly, the men all rose to go outside, Julian with them. Just before they left, Dick turned back toward Paul. Like a small child, his hopes and thoughts raced.

"Here, Paul. You take this and get yourself some new boots and things for school—whatever you need," Dick grandly offered and put a wad of twenty-dollar bills into Paul's outstretched hand.

"Thanks, Daddy," Paul replied eagerly, as he took the money and stuffed it into a pocket. *Wow!* Paul was amazed. He envisioned new hip boots, candy, cookies, pop and a hundred other little things he had seen in the stores. He grinned widely and sat back in a chair to count the money.

Dick went back to the door, beaming broadly. "See ya later,

boy," he called to Paul, and disappeared into the dark of the open porch door.

About an hour later, Julian returned. He glanced at Paul, sitting in an easy chair and working on a model car, but didn't say anything. Paul returned the look and, finding nothing forthcoming about his father and uncle, settled back to gluing the car parts together. The wind outside had picked up and rain had begun to fall—together they made quite a racket, as they beat and tore at the house.

At ten o'clock, Paul said goodnight to Julian and Mary. Julian only grunted, but Mary looked up. As she said goodnight, she smiled extra sweetly, as though she sensed that Paul might need a little extra show of affection tonight. Paul paused and warmly smiled back, before leaving the room. He had become rather fond of Mary, and appreciated the small, motherly touches of warmth she introduced into his otherwise austere life.

The rain was still beating against Paul's bedroom window when he woke up at midnight. It wasn't the rain that stirred him from slumber, however. His bedroom shared a wall with the living room, and it was the sounds from there that had disturbed him: someone or several people were talking loudly, almost shouting. Paul crawled over closer to the wall, to hear better.

Dick Surikov had stayed late at the Idle Hour. By the time Julian left, Dick was getting pretty loaded. He eventually got into an argument with his brother and left, heading out into the darkness of night, to visit the homes of some local friends.

After drinking some more there, Dick was in sad shape.

The rain soaked his clothes, and he had stumbled and fell into mud puddles several times. In all, he was quite a mess.

He knocked at three houses, to try to get out of the wind and rain and go to sleep. At the first house no one answered, even though someone was home; at the other two, the door was slammed in his face after the occupants saw who it was. By the time he reached the Golodoffs', Dick had lost his coat and cap, and had mislaid his watch and wallet somewhere. He was thoroughly confused, and tears streaked his mud-splashed face.

Julian had just gotten to sleep when Dick first banged on the door. Julian tried to ignore the noise for a few minutes, hoping whoever it was would go away, but they didn't. Cursing, he went to the door and found Dick standing there, drenched from the rain, blubbering something about "no place t'go" and "everybody says go 'way."

At first, anger from being disturbed flared in Julian's chest; a peaceful Sunday night and now this. Then the anger quickly left, as he viewed the shivering human form in front of him. *Damn,* he chided himself, as he opened the door to let Dick in, *why can't I just slam it in his face like others do?*

Dick half fell inside as Julian closed the door behind him. "Didn' know where t'go," Dick rambled, half-crying, half-stammering. "Th' wouldn' lemme in." He paused as Julian led him into the kitchen to sit on a chair, where his clothes could drip freely on the floor. "Watch… put m'watch someplace… don' know where. Gone."

"Where's your cap and coat?" Julian asked, as he set the coffee pot on the stove.

Dick looked down at his muddy, wet clothes and put a wavering hand to his head. "Don' know… gone… maybe fell off someplace… kinda cold." He shivered and started to cry again, then stopped. "You got somethin' warm t'drink… maybe somethin' t'eat, too? Ain't had n'food all day." He looked childlike up at Julian, an imploring smile on his face.

"Yeah, just a minute." Julian opened the refrigerator to fix a sandwich.

After coffee and a sandwich, Dick started to calm down a bit. Julian asked him where his money was and why he didn't buy something to eat. Dick couldn't remember where his money was; he thought he had left it with somebody, but he wasn't sure. Then he decided that someone had stolen it, and he started to get noisy, and make flourishes of anger and threat against his imaginary enemy. Julian immediately shushed him sternly, as a father admonishes a small child, and he quietened down.

While Julian got out some blankets, to make a bed for Dick on the couch, he wondered how Paul had ever come out such a decent boy, when he'd had to grow up over in Ichinski with a father like this. His thoughts rambled to his own childhood village, as he pictured himself playing out on the grassy hills, at the beach and in the homes of other villagers—and he knew the answer to his question. In his mind, he could see small Paul likewise playing on the grassy hills and beaches of his village, and he could also see Paul running to the homes of neighbors, to escape from troubles at home, and for another source of companionship. *Yes,* he thought, as he helped Dick lie down on the couch, *Paul survived like I did, and as many village kids do: by help from neighbors and relatives—and by learning to swallow your anger and wait patiently for the day when you could be master of your own home.*

"You're good t'me, Julian... I won' f'get. You good man... I..."

"Just be quiet and go to sleep," Julian interrupted. "We'll see about your stuff in the morning. It's someplace." *Out in a mud puddle, I'll bet,* Julian imagined.

He turned to shut off the light, but Dick stopped him by rolling out of bed.

"Gotta say m'prayers," he mumbled, as he knelt by the couch, shivering in his underwear. "Never f'get m'prayers."

In a low voice, and with the ease of practiced years, Dick rattled out a brief prayer, in mixed Aleut and Russian.

Julian stood with his hand resting on the doorway near the light switch, thoughtfully regarding the scene before him. A rather twisted one, Julian reflected, with this confused man clinging to the old ways, probably not understanding half of what he was saying or why, but doing as he had learned as a child, never questioning his actions. *Probably never been Outside, to see what things are like out there.*

This last thought stuck with him, as he hastily remembered his years during WWII, when his village was forced to evacuate, under threat of Japanese occupation, and his people were moved to Southeast Alaska until the war was over. He had even joined the Army, because he thought he was somehow helping to protect his village. Instead, he fought only discrimination by his comrades, and boredom from the menial tasks he was assigned. It had been a real eye-opener about the Outside. But, some things he had learned were good, and he had decided to work hard to achieve them for himself and his family. And so, here he was in Biorka, struggling.

Dick had crossed himself and was trying to get up and in bed. Julian almost had to catch him once, but Dick finally made it alone.

Once he settled, Julian turned out the light and walked past Paul and Peter's room, wondering if Paul had woken up. He paused momentarily, then went on.

Paul heard Julian's footsteps pause at the door then continue. His curiosity was stirred by the hesitation, but his thoughts about what he had heard in the previous twenty minutes were too overpowering to let anything new enter.

He had woken up just after Julian opened the front door, the pounding having stirred him. At first, the conversation had been a hazy background to the dream in which he had been deeply immersed. In the dream, his father seemed to be unhappy with him for playing at the beach. Gradually, his playing at the beach faded, and what remained was just his father being unhappy.

His father. What was his dad doing here? Immediately, his mind cleared.

Paul rolled to the side of the bed and pressed his ear against the wall. Sure enough, it was his dad talking, but… he was also crying. He was drunk again.

Paul pulled back away from the wall and flopped his head on the pillow. For a long time he just lay there, not really thinking, and not really listening to the voices he could now hear more distinctly. He had been through this all before, so the blubbering and childlike behavior wasn't new. This time, though, he was thinking about Julian and Mary, Peter and all the other people who had seen his father stumbling out in the rain that night, falling in the mud and knocking on doors for refuge and food.

Paul was thinking about himself, too. What image would these people have of him? How could he meet them on the boardwalk or in a store (or at the breakfast table), and look them in the eye, without shame and tears distorting his face? How could he now make them see the real Paul? Not the son of a drunkard, but Paul the boy, who was struggling hard just to survive in this alien town… and to be a good Aleut, despite it all. These thoughts encumbered Paul's mind, as he lay listlessly on his bed, fighting back tears and the desperate thoughts of drastic measures he might take to avoid the morrow.

But, like the inevitable tomorrow, sleep finally came.

Dick was to leave for Ichinski the next day. When Paul came home after school, his dad was there waiting.

Paul gave him back the $240 from the night before. He asked for it, saying that he needed it for supplies. Paul wondered where the rest of the $4,200 from the check had gone, but he didn't ask.

As usual when sober, Dick was quiet and inoffensive. He thanked Julian for the "hospitality", and left without a word to Paul.

Paul watched him leave, as he had so many times before, wishing that somehow his dad would give him some recognition as a son: a "'bye", or at least a nod. But, of course, nothing was offered. With tears welling in his eyes, Paul turned and went into his room.

17
Trade-Off

Catherine

That same Friday after school, Catherine, Ruth and Alice were walking home along the front boardwalk, chatting merrily. It had been a good day, especially since it was the end of the quarter, and that had finished up almost all of the graduation requirements for the girls. Each had half a credit yet to earn, and it was almost impossible not to get that, so school was effectively complete for them. However, they would have to wait until May to graduate, since the formal graduation exercise was held then. Cal and Mark would also be graduating; the five of them made up the senior class—the biggest yet—and everyone in town was looking forward to that event.

So, as the girls left the school building, they had cause to get extraordinarily silly and have a good time, as they progressed toward home, catching a smile of sympathy from passing adults. In their looseness, they even continued their antics in front of the older boys standing around the Sally Ann, and bantered with them about their behavior, something they would rarely do otherwise.

"Hey, you gals gonna go to the dance tonight?" one of the

boys called out.

"Oh, I don't know," Ruth giggled. "Why? You got some big plans, or something?"

"Well, you three act like you're already loaded. Just thought it might be worth it to see you there!"

"You never know about us, now, do you?" Ruth retorted, and all of the girls broke into laughter.

Then, with the boys calling out wisecracks, the girls continued on their way.

After passing a few houses, Alice suddenly quietened down and, with a quick motion, hushed the other girls. "It's Les," Alice whispered.

The girls sobered up, but broke down again in a moment. By that time, Les, a tall, young man with a slight swagger to his walk, had reached them.

"Hi, Les," Ruth called out.

"Hi, Ruth, Catherine. Hello, Alice," Les addressed her separately.

"Hello," Alice replied, coyly smiling.

"What's with you gals? You look like you're tanked already."

Ruth and Catherine giggled. Alice laughed: "It's just that the quarter is over; now all we gotta do is wait it out until graduation. We're honestly done right now, almost."

Les gave them all a smirking once over. "And then you're out on your own, eh?" Les Kabinoff had quit school when he was sixteen, four years earlier. "Well, good luck!" he laughed, sarcastically.

He then turned to Alice, quietly; "You wanna go out for a

few beers tonight?"

Alice smiled at him. "If you go to the dance for a while, first. Okay?"

Les paused, then agreed. "I gotta go now. See ya." He continued on his way toward the cannery.

Alice watched him walk away, then turned back as Catherine tugged at her coat sleeve. "Let's go."

The girls continued on home. Ruth chatted as usual, but Catherine noticed that Alice seemed lost in a separate world of thought. After they had said goodbye to Ruth, Catherine decided to ask Alice about Les.

"You really like that guy, huh?" Catherine asked, after they had walked in silence for a bit.

Alice didn't answer at first. "Yeah, I really do," she finally replied.

Personally, Catherine didn't care for him. Les seemed… well, strange. He was quiet mostly, and seemed nice, but other times he was explosive and had a reputation for starting a lot of fights. Les also drank quite a lot, which Catherine didn't like, but then Alice did too when she was with him. They often got into bad arguments, but Alice and Les always seemed to get back together.

Alice had started dating him in November, when he came back to town on a crab boat. His family lived here and had a reputation for drinking and violence. Some said that Les's brother had shot Michael Hoff on purpose, two years ago, when they were out hunting, but it was never proven. Anyway, there were several such incidents in the Kabinoff family history, and it scared Catherine. But it didn't seem to bother Alice.

"You going to marry him?" Catherine blurted out at last.

Alice hesitated. "Maybe. I think he might ask me tonight. I got a feeling." She turned, smiling slyly at Catherine.

It amazed Catherine how much older Alice looked than Ruth or herself. Alice had always seemed more mature for her age, probably because she had to shift for herself, since her mother's divorce when Alice was ten. But, as Catherine looked at her just then, Alice seemed a lot older than Catherine had ever imagined.

"I thought you said this fall that you wanted to get away from here—go to Anchorage and get a job; have a big time out there? Now you want to get married? I suppose that means kids and working at the cannery, too, huh?" Catherine's voice had taken on a sharp edge, and it didn't go unnoticed.

"Yeah, that's what I said this fall," Alice shot back. "So, I changed my mind. Now I've met Les, I can see something steady ahead for me. Sure, I could go to Anchorage, get a job and play around—that's what my mom does. But when I get old like her, and I ain't so pretty, and the guys don't come around anymore, then what? Huh? Then, I'm nowhere." She fell silent for a moment, thinking.

"Hell, I know Les ain't the greatest—I guess he's pretty rough sometimes—but he's a good worker. He'll build a house for me, and he's buying a boat next summer. That means I'd have a future for myself… Not like my mom."

The girls walked on in silence, watching the rough boards of the boardwalk, as they lifted slightly and fell with each step. "I never thought of it that way, Alice," Catherine finally answered.

"Well, kid, I been knocked around enough. For you, graduating from high school is a big deal; for me, it's just something to do until I find something secure—and I think Les is it. I'm not gonna let him go if I can help it. I don't care if he's a little rough with me, as long as he gives me and my kids a home and takes care of us. I heal fast, anyway."

Alice fell silent, and Catherine's thoughts raced with what she had just heard. She couldn't help glancing up at the fading bruise on Alice's cheek, either. *My God, is Alice truly that desperate?*

Or, maybe she's not desperate; maybe she's smart. Maybe life is just a lot of hard knocks and bruises, whatever their source. This conclusion chilled Catherine deeply, and she felt small and thin under her heavy parka.

They reached Alice's house and stopped.

Alice turned to Catherine and, with a smile, asked: "See ya at the dance tonight?"

"Oh, yeah, I'll be there," Catherine agreed, weakly.

Alice gave her a wink and went inside. Catherine pulled her parka closer about her and hurried on to her own house.

That night, before the dance was over, Alice pulled Catherine aside and told her that she and Les had set the wedding date, for the Saturday after school was out. Catherine had difficulty summoning up some realistic squeals of delight, but she didn't think Alice noticed.

Throughout the following week, Alice acted as though she

were on a cloud. All she could talk about were her plans with Les: where the house was to be built, what the wedding would be like, even the names of their unborn children.

Ruth and the other girls were all caught up in her euphoria. Although Catherine tried to join in, she could only mimic their enthusiasm. Daily, Catherine sensed a wall building between her and Alice. She didn't fully understand it, yet she knew it had to do with Alice's decision.

But, perhaps it wasn't really that Alice acted so different, after all—she was still fun to be with. Maybe it was that Catherine had this feeling that Alice was lying about how she truly felt about getting married and settling down. On the other hand, maybe Alice was right: maybe that was the smartest—indeed, the only—thing to do. It was the choice of nearly every woman in Biorka to marry and have kids. Maybe all that talk by Mrs. Irving, about choices and decisions, only applied to women on the Outside, in big cities, or something. Or, maybe it was all a lot of garbage—someone's wild dreams.

All this thinking only confused Catherine more. She couldn't find any right or wrong, or anything that made sense.

After a couple of days, she grew used to the change in her friend and began simply accepting her as she was: no whys or anything. That is, until that next Saturday night.

18
Consequence

Catherine

That weekend started out not being much for Catherine, just house-cleaning with her mother on Saturday morning, and doing some grocery shopping that afternoon at the company store. That evening, after dinner, she luxuriated in a long, hot bath and took time to put up her hair, trim her fingernails and enjoy other small luxuries of time. After watching some TV, she went to bed and looked at a screen magazine she had bought earlier at the store. It was 12:15 a.m. when she finally laid it down.

Just as she was reaching over to turn out the light, a gunshot rang out sharply, as if almost next door. She jumped involuntarily from the surprise, and had hardly recovered when two more shots were fired. Now Catherine sat up in bed, wide awake.

She heard her dad and mother talking and stirring. Sometimes in the winter, after confining days of snow and cold, some men would take to shooting a rifle or pistol outdoors during a drinking bout, to let off some steam. Catherine had decided it was just some show-off this time, too, and was settling back under her blankets, when she heard someone yelling a few houses away. It was difficult to tell from where, with the wind blowing like it was.

Then there was another shot—not as loud as the others, but muffled, as if inside a house.

This time, she threw the covers back and slipped out of bed. Catherine was disturbed; it didn't sound like the usual drunken spree. A light at the neighbor's window went on, and under her bedroom door she also saw light from the living room flashing on. Someone was up.

Opening her door, Catherine saw her father stepping into his rubber boots and tucking his pajamas in. As he stood up to swing on his heavy coat, he caught sight of Catherine standing in the doorway. He stopped for a moment, then continued buttoning his coat. "Probably just some of the fellas got a little carried away." Opening the door, he ventured outside.

Catherine watched his outline through a window, until he disappeared. She stood still, listening to the wind, and heard nothing at first.

Then there followed shouts and a woman shrieking. More excited voices, and someone ran by their house. This was too much to take. Something bad had happened.

As she started for the door, with her slippers on and clutching a blanket, her mother's voice rang out: "Catherine! Where are you going?"

Pausing only for a second, to gather strength enough to disobey, she replied, "I'm going to find Papa," and dashed outside, as her mother commanded her to come back.

It was pitch-black outside, and she nearly fell in her rush

to escape. Once safely outside, she stopped to listen and quiet her pounding heart. Over to her right, toward town and along the boardwalk, there was a light; she heard voices, too, and hurried in that direction. The wind was biting cold, but at least it wasn't raining at the moment. She passed one, two houses… There was a light on at Alice's house.

Two people came rushing out, then scurried around, back into the darkness: Ted and Elizabeth Kozloff, with whom Alice was staying. Quickly, sensing their urgency, Catherine followed, stumbling along until she suddenly emerged upon a nearby house, with all the lights blazing brightly. At first, she couldn't place it. Then, as she stepped onto the porch, she realized it was Les Kabinoff's house. Excited voices came from inside. With her heart pounding, Catherine slipped into the house.

Five people were in the front room, three of them bending over something on the floor. The smell of gunpowder hung in the air. Back in a dimly lit corner, she noticed a sixth person sitting on the floor, his head resting on his knees. It was Les.

He was breathing deeply and slowly. His head came up and his glazed stare met Catherine's eyes. He was obviously drunk, but his eyes were… empty.

"Catherine!" a surprised voice sang out her name. She jerked around and saw her father, having stood up from tending what lay on the floor. "What are you doing here?" he demanded.

Before Catherine could answer, her gaze dropped from her father's face to his hands: a bloodstained towel dangled from one of them. Her gaze fell further to the object on the floor: it was a body.

Elizabeth moved back slightly from the person on the floor. There, cradled in her arms, was Alice.

Only, it wasn't the shining, bright face of the Alice from school; it was the face of a pale store mannequin, with wet, black hair straggling over her eyes. A red stain slowly spread through the towel Elizabeth was pressing to Alice's head.

Wordlessly, Catherine mouthed Alice's name. She couldn't talk or move. Finally, she looked up sharply and her gaze riveted on the crouching figure in the corner. *Les! He shot her! My God!*

"Catherine!" Her father's words brought her attention back to the situation. "Either get out or help."

She looked down at the limp, bleeding figure on the floor and, without thinking, responded: "I'll help."

"Get some more towels for Elizabeth. John and I are going for the nurse. Marvin, you keep your eyes on Les over there. We'll be right back." The two men disappeared outside.

Catherine hurried past Les into the bathroom and, after rummaging, found a stack of towels. As she squatted down to give them to Elizabeth, she couldn't help asking: "Is she going to live?"

Elizabeth angrily responded: "How the hell do I know? Ask that young buck over there in the corner! This is his job tonight."

As she pulled the towel away to be replaced by a fresh one, the wound was exposed, and Catherine saw a thick mat of bloodied hair, with a small, pencil-sized hole oozing blood. Elizabeth caught Catherine's awestruck look and softly stated, "Not very pretty, is it?" as she pressed the fresh towel to the wound.

Helplessly, Catherine knelt at Elizabeth's side, watching Alice's labored breathing. She felt something warm and sticky in her hand and, looking down, saw that without thinking she had picked up one of Alice's hands, and was clasping it in her own.

Catherine laid her other hand on top of Alice's limp fingers and squeezed them. Tears now streaming from her eyes, Catherine closed them tightly to staunch the flow and lowered her head, hanging on tightly to the stained hand of her dying friend.

By five o'clock that morning it was all over: Alice never regained consciousness. She simply slowed down and finally stopped breathing. They moved her on a stretcher to the nurse's quarters, where injections and special compresses were administered, but to no avail. There was no blood available in town for transfusion, and she was bleeding too rapidly to keep what she had left in her system.

The Coast Guard was alerted, and a military helicopter from Adak was ready to go as soon as daylight and the weather permitted, but it never took off. Alice was left to fight her battle by herself, but it was hopeless from the start—maybe even from the very start of Alice's life, Catherine would conclude during the next few days.

And, so the night ended. Alice was dead.

The town mayor sat up with Les in his house, until the

State Troopers could fly in the next afternoon.

Although Catherine tried, she could not get to sleep, so sat up talking with her mother. At about eight in the morning, she finally fell asleep from exhaustion.

School on Monday was hard for Catherine. She and Ruth fell crying into each other's arms immediately upon entering the school corridor. For a lot of other kids, and teachers, it was hard to concentrate on schoolwork.

In Mrs. Irving's class that day, much of the time was spent discussing what had happened: Les and Alice arguing in the bar, him pulling Alice out of bed later that night, and threatening her aunt and uncle with the gun; the shots at his house… Mrs. Irving said it would be "good to get it out in the open", and Catherine agreed.

By Tuesday it was easier for everyone, and soon school was almost back to normal. That afternoon, when school was over, Alice was buried out in the cemetery near the lagoon, amidst the tilting, white Russian Orthodox crosses, which refused to stay put in the frost-heaved tundra soil. They loaded her coffin onto a flat-bed truck, and hauled it the short distance along the chuck-holed lagoon road.

Several adults squeezed into the cab while others, including Ruth and Catherine, walked along behind the truck. A bunch of exuberant adolescents, taking advantage of the opportunity for a joyride, swarmed aboard and, with festive air, rode out the jostling trip sitting atop Alice's plain wooden coffin.

At the cemetery, a few words were said in Russian Orthodox prayer by the postmaster, who was an elder of the church—since the priest came only once a month, on his rounds of service—then the coffin was lowered into the partially frozen earth. Then, with yells and shouts, the kids merrily chased the truck, as it bounced back to town.

Alice's mother flew in on the Goose that morning, and was taking a return mail flight out in the afternoon. Just after she left the cemetery in Ted and Elizabeth's pickup, and as the first clods of dirt rang hollow on the coffin lid, the plane roared in low over the rooftops on a landing approach, and dropped out of sight as the engines throttled back.

Catherine and Ruth stayed behind and—with the exception of Old George, to whom the town's grave-digging duty fell—were the only ones left at the cemetery.

It was late in the afternoon, and the sun had passed behind the near hills to the southwest, bringing a sudden cooling of the air. The scattered patches of snow crunched loudly beneath their feet, as the two took a few tentative steps toward the grave. Both girls stood without speaking, the utter silence of that lonely place being broken only by the resonant thud of the spadefuls of earth which tumbled down upon the coffin. Neither of them could speak, torn between their sense of duty to their departed friend and their growing uneasiness of being where they were.

Finally, with a shudder, Catherine turned and grabbed Ruth's arm, firmly. Pulling them closer together, she whispered, hoarsely: "Let's go.

19
Plans

Cal

It was a warm April Sunday, and a truly fine day—another special day in Biorka, when the sun was out and the wind had ceased.

It seemed as if the entire town was alive. There was activity everywhere: boats moving in the harbor; people in groups, passing on the boardwalk; kids on three-wheelers and motorcycles, buzzing through the bumpy streets; and small knots of adults and children, strolling along trails up the hill and by the beach.

Even the songbirds were back, flitting from bush to bush. Startled coveys of ptarmigan on the hillsides flushed occasionally, revealing their newly molted, patchy-brown feathers, as they swooped away. Alder buds were ready to burst into leaf, and the willows had sent forth the first fuzzy nubbins, which children prize so dearly. Parka squirrels chattered noisily, as they scurried from burrow to burrow, and a few bumblebees droned loudly, as they sought the first tundra flowers of the year. Like the clear, pure sound of a bell, this sunny day seemed to announce the beginning of spring, and played a prelude to the rhythms of summer.

At the boat launch and storage area near the cannery ruins, a fishing boat was on the ways, and being lowered into the water. Another boat was being jacked along sideways, to get into position for the next launching. Soon, the first schools of salmon would pass by, and there was a flurry of activity to prepare the boats for the new season.

Cal was with his dad and uncle, working on the *Panof*, taking advantage of the pleasant weather to paint the hull of the boat. They were third in line for launching, and wanted to have the anti-fouling bottom paint on and dry when their turn came up. Other fishermen on either side of the *Panof* were also preparing to launch, and a good deal of jesting and serious conversation alike went on between the men.

Cal was under the hull near the keel, giving that section a final scraping, in preparation for the paint. It was a hard and dirty job, because the work had to be done in such an awkward position. Hence, this task traditionally went to the youngest member of a boat's crew. But Cal didn't mind; it felt good to be outside again, working hard and getting dirty.

Basketball was over, and the season had gone well. All of school was about over, and now Cal was turning his thoughts to fishing and the summer.

Gradually, his mind drifted off to past summers and favorite memories: days out on the sparkling, blue sea; the thrill of seeing the first fish of a set, as the big winch hauled in the net; and the seemingly endless number of salmon which spilled onto the deck, as the net's purse-lines were pulled.

The work and the reward—Cal knew and loved them both.

So far, he had managed to put away $25,000 over the last two seasons, and still had plenty to spend on a motorcycle, a stereo and clothes. He loved fishing, and eagerly looked forward to the coming season.

The hum of the men's conversation continued nearby, and Cal worked on, scraping and dreaming. Slowly, though, his thoughts were pulled back to the present, as he became aware that his name kept popping up in the conversation. *Yes, there it was again.* Cal's interest picked up sharply, and he strained to catch every word said.

"Yep," Cal's father was saying, "we figure that with Walt, Cal and me working the two boats this summer," (*What's that about two boats?* Cal wondered) "we'll be able to buy that crab boat in Homer this September, and be set to crab through February next year, at least. The three of us should be able to handle it alright," he concluded.

Cal stopped scraping, his arm poised. *Hold on, I don't get it. I wasn't planning to work all summer! Two boats must mean me being steady crew on one—not changing off with Walter, like before.*

John Gustafson's voice interrupted his thoughts: "Well, the boy should be out there regular. Time he got steady on somethin'."

"Yeah, he always was crazy 'bout fishin'," Walter spoke up. "Seems like it's all he wanted to do in the summer, when he was a little tyke: be out there somewhere, gettin' some fish."

"Looks like he's gonna get plenty of that soon, with your plans!" John wrinkled his face up into a wide grin as he spoke.

The other men joined in the joke, and Cal caught further

fragments of conversation: "see if he can get fish in a net like he does basketballs" and "that Catherine'll make a good wife," could be heard through the laughter and hawing.

Cal went deaf with the anger that swelled up from within. "Who do they think they are," he spat out, in muttered tones, "figuring out my whole life for me?!" He took several savage jabs at the barnacles with his scraper. *Nobody asked me. They just take me for granted—like a kid, he grimaced.* More jabs.

He missed the boat and scraped his knuckles on the barnacles. "Damn!" he muttered, as he put his bleeding hand to his mouth.

Maybe I don't want to fish or crab, he thought, defiantly. *Maybe I'd rather...* Here, his rebellion stopped for a second... then picked up: *Maybe I'd rather go to college and play basketball!*

"Yeah," he mumbled, and smiled with pleasure at his brilliance.

Cal started scraping again, and this new thought rambled about in his head for a while, as he recalled Coach Irving's encouragement to seek a scholarship at an Alaskan college, as well as the good time he'd had in Anchorage, on the business class trip. He found that he kind of enjoyed being out there, where a lot was happening. And, the foreman at the manufacturing plant he'd apprenticed with that week, said that Cal showed promise in some kind of business, because he dug right in and stayed with his assigned task.

Maybe I could get a job in Anchorage—and have a good time there! Going out, dating women, having parties... Heck, if Mrs. Irving pushed the idea for girls, then it ought to be a snap for a guy like me!

While Cal played with this new dream, he scraped harder and faster until, suddenly, he was done.

"Ho, you act like you enjoy that job, Cal!" his uncle broke in. Grinning, he added: "Come on, let's get the paint and finish 'er up."

Slightly confused by the abrupt shift from dream to reality, Cal blinked and rose to his feet, as Walter slapped a hand on his shoulder. Cal managed a slight smile, and made a motion of wiping some dirt from his face, to give himself a chance to recover. He walked back to where the other men were working, to get the paint, then he and Walter set about painting.

As he worked, Cal had to admit to himself that now he was really confused. *Why am I so angered by all the talk about the plans being made for me?* After all, fishing was all he had ever wanted to do. For as long as he could remember, he had spent all of his summers outdoors, stalking the streams to throw rocks at migrating salmon when he was a little guy, or snagging them off of the cannery docks when he was older. He just thought and dreamed about fish all summer long. And, when he could go out on the boat with his dad and uncle, boy, was he one happy kid! It was in his blood, his dad had used to say to him, and Cal believed it was, too. So, why was he upset? It couldn't be the idea of fishing—he was sure of that.

Maybe it was because it was all done without him, and without asking him if it was okay, or if he minded putting in more time. Maybe that was it.

Or, maybe it was also because he had tucked away in the

back of his mind all that Coach Irving had said, about college and basketball. Lord knew how much basketball meant to him, and he would do anything to keep it going… And, the trip to Anchorage… that had been a good time; all of those things he saw and did were like candy canes hanging on a Christmas tree, tantalizing him.

"Okay, that's it," Walter's voice broke in, "let's get 'er ready for the dolly; we're next, after the *Puffin*."

Cal grabbed his brush and paint can, and headed back to the rails, where his dad was getting ready to jack the boat along.

"Get some grease on those rails, Cal," his dad pointed to the cans in the pickup; "we gotta be ready slide 'er down when it's time." And he broke into a wide, kid-like grin, which Cal knew and understood well: the boat in the water and ready for the sea!

Cal grinned back, turned and took off at a trot, back to the truck.

20
Plans

Catherine

A few days later, Catherine ran into Cal during a class change. She had been thinking about something Ruth had told her, and she wasn't aware that the person she almost collided with was Cal until, surprised, she looked up.

"Oh! Cal!" she exclaimed, as she put her hand to her chest and smiled in relief. "I didn't see you."

From his reaction, it was obvious that Cal had also been deep in thought and was similarly surprised. "Ho, you surprised me, too!"

He grinned, then turned more somber. "I guess I wasn't watching where I was going." He looked down at the floor and scuffed the carpet with his foot.

"Uh, haven't seen you around," he noted, looking up at Catherine.

"No, I've been sort of busy," she slowly replied. "I've had a lot to think about."

"Yeah, I know what you mean." Then, he added: "Can't wait to get out of this place."

The warning bell rang, and both hurried to their respective classes.

As she went in and sat down, Catherine thought about her brief encounter with Cal. He seemed a little different lately, she admitted. It had briefly crossed her mind before that she and Cal hadn't gone out for the last several weeks, but it hadn't stuck in her mind as odd. Now, however, she was very conscious that she had hardly seen him at all anywhere, in school or otherwise. They had a couple of classes together, but even there he had been aloof.

Cal was a rather quiet person, to be sure, but there was something deeper to it now, and this encounter proved it. He acted like he wasn't there—as if the near-collision only briefly brought him out of a shell, into which he immediately withdrew. What was it he had said? "I know what you mean?" He had a lot to think about, too? Heck, Cal never took the time to think about anything! He always had an answer right away—or, at least, made you think that he did.

Catherine let these thoughts roll around for a while. *What could he be thinking about so hard?* she wondered. But, she couldn't come up with an answer, so her thoughts drifted on to other matters.

After school, Ruth was right there to grab Catherine by the sleeve and pull her aside.

"Alright, what is it? You're sure acting strange!"

"We-e-l-l-l-l," Ruth drew the word out, "we're going to see somebody tonight."

"Oh, is that so? And, who is that supposed to be?"

"Frannie Gustafson."

"Frannie? You mean Molly's niece?" Catherine knew perfectly well who Frannie was; she just wanted time to clear her thoughts. Frannie had gone out to Anchorage and college for two years, and had just flown home because her mother was seriously ill.

A brief flutter of excitement rose within Catherine. They were supposed to see Georgiana, Ruth's sister, during vacation, but she never came. Now, here was another chance to talk with someone.

"I saw her last night, and she wants us to come over tonight, to talk about... you know... *our plan*!" Ruth's face beamed.

Catherine looked at her friend, all aglow with the excitement of stepping closer to a cherished dream. While Catherine rarely talked about Ruth's crazy idea, Ruth was constantly letting Catherine in on some little detail of her latest scheme, or showing her a college catalog the library had just received. Ruth wore her dream on her sleeve, but Catherine hid hers, perilously suspended between heart and mind.

That night, at seven-thirty, the two girls went over to see Frannie.

She ushered them in with a warmth and casualness that Catherine was not used to. She made them feel so at ease that they immediately struck up a lively conversation, about college and living Outside.

Two hours passed in no time at all. No matter what

question the girls asked, unrelated or silly (as Catherine thought), Frannie could answer it, and make the question seem to have been a good one. Before leaving, Catherine and Ruth had tea and cookies.

"Well, what do you think?" Frannie asked, outright. "Are you going?"

Ruth immediately effused: "Of course! I can't wait!" She turned to grin at Catherine and squeezed her hand. "We'll have a great time together!"

Catherine tried to be more serious and keep her enthusiasm down, though it was difficult. "I don't know. Really, I don't know."

Ruth pursed her lips and mocked a pout.

"I mean, it sounds exciting to be out and doing stuff together, but… I'm scared, too." Catherine paused. "It seems like about everybody who goes out, sooner or later can't make it, and they come back." She looked imploringly at Frannie; "Except you."

"Well, it's tough, that's true. I mean, I still miss my mom and dad, and sometimes I just sit down and cry, because I'm so homesick." Frannie glanced from girl to girl. "But, somehow I pull out of it and get going again, then I wonder how I could be so silly."

She smiled and immediately became serious again. "I guess it depends on whether you truly want to go out there and try, or not. For me, I remember in grade school, seeing pictures in books and films of places and people Outside, and I remember wishing with all my heart to see a train or a cow, or to live in a big city." She paused again. "And, now I've seen all those things—and lots more, too. I just wanted that more than anything, and even though the thought of actually doing it scared the hell out of me, I always felt I would somehow be… well… empty, unless I did it."

Catherine waited, then asked: "Do you still feel empty?"

Frannie thought for a moment. "Yes and no."

Catherine looked confused.

"I mean, no because I've learned a lot about things and, more importantly, how to handle myself with other people. Strangers used to terrify me here in Biorka, because they weren't people I'd known all my life. Now it's easy for me to meet people I've never met before and, truthfully, it's a lot of fun!"

She noticed the suspicious look on Catherine's face, and continued: "Yes because… well, I've discovered that, no matter how much I learn or do, there is always something more to learn and do. There's so much in the world out there, it's hard to keep from getting confused. But, I think it's worth trying to learn and do more things." She looked at Ruth, who was intently watching, with bright eyes.

"So-o-o, I guess I always feel kind of empty, but, at the same time, I'm working at filling myself up, too." She glanced at the girls. "Understand?"

Ruth nodded an enthusiastic, "Yes," while Catherine just stared at her. There was an awkward break in the conversation.

Finally, Ruth spoke up to say that they had better be going. Catherine unfroze and told Frannie sincerely that they'd had a good time, and that talking with her had helped a lot. It all ended very warmly, and the girls were chatting gaily when they stepped out into the dark.

Frannie leaned against the door as she closed it, and paused for a moment, her hand still on the doorknob. A slight smile remained on her lips, but her eyes misted over with a brief welling up of tears, as she thought back on the events of the past few years of her life—and the ones now facing the two girls who had so innocently just stepped through the door.

After school the next day, the girls went to see George Campbell, the business teacher, who was unofficially serving as a counselor for seniors. In characteristic Biorka fashion, they quietly and haltingly told him they might be interested in attending a college, and would he help them, in case they did get interested?

Having learned his lesson last year about being over-enthusiastic, Campbell settled down to simply, but encouragingly, explain what needed to be done.

He could detect from the increasingly bewildered look on the girls' faces that the forms and procedures were confusing them. He slowly repeated what was necessary for them to do.

"Why can't we just go there and walk into the classes, like we do here?" Ruth objected. "Why do they need all these papers and stuff?" She wrinkled up her nose and pushed at the papers.

Campbell looked at Ruth's scowling, though still pretty face, and smiled encouragingly. "Because they need to know more about you," he began. "Here, everybody already knows everything about everybody, but out there nobody knows who you are. They may have never even heard of this place before!"

Thinking that this might sound too scary, he added, quickly: "They want to know more about you so they can help you be at home there, and help you decide exactly what you want to do with your life."

That didn't sound much better, so he decided to change topic: "Besides, there are a lot of organizations that will help pay for your expenses at college, and these forms are for that, too. Being an Alaskan Native is a real advantage in getting money for school. You should be sure to use the opportunity." He paused. "I wish more kids like you two would come in to see me about it," he added, somewhat wistfully. He looked at the girls.

They smiled meekly, and he could see that confusion still reigned.

"Look, you take these home to fill out—do as much as you can—then come back and I'll help, okay? But do it this week, since there is a deadline for when they have to be back at the colleges."

The girls rose and thanked him. Once in the hallway and around a corner, they both broke down in giggles of excitement. They couldn't contain themselves any longer, and gave in to the thrill of adventure.

21
Parents

Catherine

At home that night, Catherine brought out the college application and financial aid forms Mr. Campbell had given her. Her parents' first reaction was confusion.

"I don't understand, Catherine," her mother finally declared. "You mean you want to leave us?" Her face and brow wrinkled, her eyes searching Catherine for clarification.

One glance at her father's dark, brooding face, as he leaned back in his chair, with arms folded across his chest, told her that she was in for big trouble.

"Well," she began, "yes… No, I mean… It's not like that."

"What's the matter? We ain't good enough for you here?" her father spat out. "Humph!" He settled back down again. "No good comes of women going off like that. They just get stuck-up, spoiled and pregnant!"

Catherine was at a loss for words. Her throat tightened as she fought down the impulse to cry. Finally, she began: "Ruth and I want to go to college, and room together at one of the dormitories. Mr. Campbell and Mrs. Irving both say we've got good grades and should be able to do well. Besides," and she hoped that this would help ease the tension, "Mr. Campbell says that we should be able to get enough money from the Aleut Corporation and the Bureau of Indian Affairs, so it won't cost much—just for what we want to spend on extras and plane fare."

"And, where you gonna get that?" her father demanded.

"I've got my own money I worked hard for!" Catherine responded, with some heat. Now she was getting a little angry about the way her parents were reacting. *They're acting like I've got no right to use my money as I want,* she thought, bitterly.

I suppose... No, I'll say it out loud, she decided: "I suppose that if instead I had said I wanted to get married, you both would have been happy, eh?"

"Make a hell of a lot more sense," her father retorted.

Her mother spoke up: "Well, Cathy, that's what women usually do: get married and start a family. So, if you had wanted to—"

"But I *don't* want to right now," Catherine broke in. "I want to... to see some things first... do some things!"

"Like what, dear?"

"Well, like... meet other people, like I met in Anchorage, on the business class trip."

"Strangers can be dangerous sometimes, Catherine," her mother continued. "Lots of people in places like Anchorage aren't good. They have a lot of strange ideas. Makes me shiver to think about it."

"They aren't all that way; I met a lot of friendly people. But, it isn't just people: the cities have lots of things to do and see and buy. Momma, you wouldn't believe some of the stores; it's just like walking into a Sears catalog!" She smiled at the memory of the large department stores, loaded with merchandise and busy with activity.

Her mother was also thinking of memories: of the fear she felt when she visited Anchorage, several years ago; of all the bustle, and strangers, and cars hurtling about. She thought, too, of how closely she clung to her sister and aunt, as the three of them spent a day shopping. Sure, there was a lot to see and do, and the stores were marvelous, but it was also a place of fear, and she could hardly wait to get back to the peace and security of Biorka.

A silence passed and Catherine spoke up again: "If I could decide on my own to get married, and you two would say it's okay, then why can't I decide on my own to go to college, and that be okay?" She waited for an answer.

Her father spoke: "Because one makes sense and the other is stupid, that's why!" He got up from the kitchen table and sat down in the living room, to busy himself with lighting up a smoke.

Catherine turned to her mother, putting a hand on hers. "Momma?" she questioned.

Her mother said nothing, paused, then replied: "I just don't understand why you want to leave us."

"It isn't forever, you know! I'll be home for Christmas and all of summer. Besides, I'll just go for one year and see how I like it; if I don't like it, I'll stay here the next year. Anyway, it would just be two years at the most, then I'd get a degree and come back here to stay."

But, would I? Catherine wondered, not knowing if she was lying, or wishing, or whatever. "Just let me fill out these forms—Mr. Campbell says they have to be returned soon—and you think about it, okay?"

Her mother lifted her eyes to meet Catherine's. Her face had a tired, sad look and her eyes glistened with a slight moistness. She nodded her head and, with a deep sigh and a slow shaking of her head in disbelief, she rose from the table and set about some work in the kitchen.

Catherine was left sitting at the table, with the forms scattered upon it. She slowly gathered them into a neat pile and went off to her bedroom.

Late that night, the window of her bedroom was still lit, when the first drops of a rain squall started drumming against it.

Two days later, at noon break, Catherine met Cal outside on the boardwalk, and told him of her plans.

His reaction surprised her. She had expected him to be glad or angry, at least, but he showed nothing; his face was blank. It was just like when she had nearly bumped into him in the hall the other day: he seemed far-off and vacant.

"Cal!" she exploded in frustration. "Say something!"

But, Cal couldn't. He didn't know how to react or reply, because he was confronted by a situation which was completely outside his previous experience and his standard of conduct. Though his thoughts raced, he couldn't move his body to respond.

When Catherine dropped her news, he finally began to grasp why she had been so irritable, so pre-occupied in thought, these past several months. The jumble of impressions he had then all fit together now. He remembered the discussion about women, careers and choices in Mrs. Irving's class, and how Catherine had been so quiet and listened intently. After that, she and Ruth seemed to always have some kind of secret they were talking about.

He also remembered how, after Alice was shot, Catherine kept drifting back to talking about how Alice had wanted to go to Anchorage to work, and then suddenly decided wanted to stay and be a housewife. Then Les killed her. Catherine kept rambling on about Alice never having a chance, and not being able to choose.

The whole thing was a bore to Cal then, but now he understood. It all made sense. Catherine was trying to make a choice, and had finally made it. That her parents were hassling her about it helped him understand even more.

He thought back to that Sunday at the boatyard, when his dad told the other fishermen of his plans for Cal, and how upset he was about it. He understood Catherine's feelings exactly now, and he felt closer to her than ever before. Yet, he did nothing.

At first, Catherine flushed with anger at Cal. Why did he just stand there? Couldn't he see? Hadn't he noticed anything different about her these past few months? Then, looking him full in the face, searching, she grasped the meaning of those big, sad eyes of his, which seemed to be looking so meekly at her. *He does understand!*

Well, then, why doesn't he…

And finally, she realized why. He didn't know how to say the words. The words of comfort and feeling—yes, even tenderness—that she sought. They were beyond him—beyond the fisherman-basketball hero that was his usual self.

She truly felt sorry for him, and a brief wave of compassion broke over her, only to ebb quickly, as determination and pride caught hold.

Hell! She'd be damned if she would make it easy for him! If he was such a big man, then he should have the guts to at least try to come out of his shell—this image he had molded himself into—and try bridging the chasm which separated them, as they now stood facing each other on the windswept boardwalk. That was all he had to do—make an effort, come halfway—and she would do her part.

But, Cal remained silent. He was trapped by his silence, for the longer he was quiet, the harder it was to utter that first word. Thus, the opportunity for the two of them to come wholly and naturally to the aid and comfort of each other rose and faded, like a wave rolling a precious shell on a beach, only to snatch it back, when no hand reached out to grasp it.

The wave had crested, and both Cal and Catherine knew it. The inner depth their eyes had momentarily shown—the seeking, the questing—disappeared. Now, there remained only the faces of a young man and a young woman, named Cal and Catherine, meeting during a lunch break at school—that was all.

The bell split the air with its harsh clamor, and the two moved automatically toward the school building and their waiting friends.

22
Parents

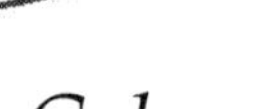

Cal

For the next two weeks, Cal was in a foul mood. He avoided Catherine, grumbled at everyone and was surly at school. He was called in by the principal once, because of a teacher's complaint. While Parkhurst lectured at length about the necessity of learning adult behavior, and the imminence of Cal's leaving the "protective cocoon of school", Cal simply sat stone-faced and stared at him.

Coach Irving went out of his way to cheerfully greet Cal, even though Cal only managed an acknowledging grunt, but Irving never pressed Cal on his behavior. Only once, when they happened to be going in the same direction down a half-empty hallway, did Irving make the offer for Cal to stop in and talk sometime… if he wished.

At home, things were a little more serious. He slept in late, was abominably slow with chores and even refused to work on the boat once. This unavoidably led to heated arguments with his father and uncle. His father threatened him with not being able to crew on the boats this summer and fall, if he didn't stop this behavior. Cal only responded by getting drunk and not coming home that night—or the next. It was a very tense situation.

One day, about the end of these two weeks, Cal came home to find a letter waiting for him. It was dinnertime and everyone had already sat down to eat, when he came in and had the letter handed to him. He glanced at the large envelope: it was from the University of Alaska, Fairbanks. Cal tossed it aside, took off his coat and sat down to eat.

There was some small conversation amongst the rest of the family, while Cal silently ate.

"What's that big envelope got in it?" Cal's father finally asked.

Cal looked up from his plate, glanced again at the manila envelope and replied: "Dunno." He knew that response would irritate his parents, and he could feel the tension building in the silence which followed.

Then, out of a combination of devilry and a desire not to get too deep into trouble, he added: "It's from some college or something." Leaning over to read the return address, he continued: "University of Alaska in Fairbanks, I guess."

Trying to avoid another scene, his mother managed a smile and a cheerful voice: "Well, why don't you open it? See what's inside."

Putting his fork down and sighing heavily, as though it were a huge task, Cal reached over and pulled the envelope to him. Opening it slowly, still chewing his food, he pulled out four sheets of paper and some folded literature about the University. He glanced at the sheets. The first was a letter, the next three forms of some kind.

He went back to the letter and began reading. About

halfway through, he suddenly stopped chewing his food. Then, toward the letter's end, he began chewing again. Finishing the letter, he thumbed through the forms. Finally, he set them all down in a pile and reached for a glass of milk.

"Well?" his father asked. "What did they say?"

Cal motioned off-handedly at the letter and leaned back against the chair. "Oh, they want me to go to school there next year. Play basketball, too, I guess." He glanced at the faces of his parents. "They say they'll give me a basketball scholarship, which will pay my room and board. Said I could probably get money to cover the rest of what I need, too. They sent these forms to be filled out."

With that, Cal stopped and faced the expected onslaught.

"Play basketball?! Hell, son, it's time you growed up! You can't make no living playing games! You're gonna have a family one of these days, and you'll hafta support 'em." The fury of Frank Larsen surprised even Cal's mother. His little brother Freddy sat frozen, with a spoon in his upraised hand.

"It's just a letter, saying I could go if I wanted to," Cal protested.

"I don't give a damn what it is," his dad broke in. "You ain't going off to no college to play around, while the rest of us stay here to work."

"It isn't just to play around," Cal objected; "I'd be taking classes, too—stuff that would do me some good. Maybe there would be something different I'd like to do for a living: some kind of business in machinery, or stores, or somethin'."

Frank Larsen ran his fingers through his thinning, silvered-black hair and leaned forward on his elbows. "I've got plans for you, to work here on the boats with us: me and your uncle Walter… and Freddy, too." Freddy looked up, his eyes shining brightly over the rim of the glass of milk he was drinking.

Now Cal's anger rose, and with sudden venom spat out: "There you go, making my mind up for me; telling me what I'm going to do with my life! You never asked me if I wanted to work full-time this summer, or crabbing this winter; you never thought about it. You just make your plans for me, tell everybody else and then expect me to be happy with it all!"

Cal was in deep, now. He knew it, but he couldn't back down; he was too proud. He paused to gather strength for the next assault. "Maybe I don't want to be like you, and fish all my life. Maybe I'd rather work on an oil rig, or in an office… live in a big city… maybe even play basketball for money. Coach Irving thinks I'm pretty good, you know."

Silence.

"There's other ways to live, besides here, fishing."

Cal's dad leaned back into his chair and looked at his son, almost a man now, wondering: *What's got into him? He's acting like a little kid, when he should act like a grown-up!* He felt as though he didn't know this person at all.

"I don't understand you, Cal," his father began, in a moderate voice: "all your life you wanted to fish, like me and Walter—that's all you ever talked about. Isn't that right, Liz?"

Cal's mother nodded her head.

"Now, we got a chance this summer to contract out a company boat for Walter, and you and Freddy can change off crewing both boats. That way, we can make really good money, buy that crab boat in Homer and get to crabbing, all fall and winter. You gotta help out on this, or we can't do it." He paused. "We need you here, Cal, not off someplace playing with a ball."

He pushed his chair back and rose from the table. "So, you just throw those papers away and forget that nonsense. You understand?"

Cal looked at his father, grabbed the forms and stalked off to his room.

As Cal slammed his bedroom door, he could hear his mother's soothing voice, trying to quiet his father down.

I don't care, he fumed; *he can stay mad forever, as far as I'm concerned. He just orders me around all the time. He never treats me like he should!*

However, as he sat thinking, he began to cool off, and he had to admit that this wasn't quite true. His father was pretty fair with him most of the time—tough, but fair.

Well, so what? That doesn't make any difference…

Maybe I really would like to go to college: play ball, learn a new occupation and have a good time in the city. Yeah, maybe I would like to do that! After all, there's no harm in trying; if I didn't like it, I could always come back home.

Cal sat on his bed, pondering the freshness of this new reasoning, while absent-mindedly fingering through the forms and looking at the brochure pictures.

Gradually, his interest picked up, and he soon found himself struggling through the forms spread out on his bed. He filled in as much as he could, then lay staring at them.

Finally, he remembered Coach Irving—he had said to stop

in anytime—and decided to take the forms to him. *After all, it was his idea that I could play college ball! Maybe he's the one who got the University to send me this offer in the first place!*

Intrigued by the complexity of these thoughts, Cal grabbed up his papers, shoved them on a shelf and got ready for bed.

His last thoughts, before sleep that night, were of a basketball game in college, where he was the star. Soon, he was asleep.

23
Outside

Cal

Cal was right: Coach Irving could help him finish the application forms.

Cal was a little surprised about one thing, though. He thought Irving would be very happy to find out he was going to the University to play ball—at least, Cal wanted to make it look like he was going for certain. However, Irving just took it in stride, with that easygoing manner of his, and took the forms. "Sure, let's see what you've got here." And, they set about filling them out.

Later, Cal was returning from the post office, where he had dropped off his forms to the University. The wind was gusting, just enough to set up dark, horseshoe-shaped movements playing across the surface of the harbor, and to excite the gulls into noisy antics, as they rose on the uplift afforded by the air.

As he walked along the beach boardwalk, Cal watched the racing water movements and the wheeling gulls. He felt somehow envious of the freedom they displayed—going here and there, disappearing and reappearing—while here he was, feeling trapped, not knowing what he wanted to do, but somehow forced into doing something, at least.

"Hey, Cal!"

The sound of his name and the figure of a young man approaching from a connecting boardwalk diverted his attention. It was Wayne Olsen, a fisherman of about thirty-five years old, whom Cal had known all his life.

"Whatcha doin'?" asked the slim, young man dressed in rubber boots, green rain-gear, and wearing his Greek fisherman's cap, pulled jauntily to one side. A mustache adorned his upper lip, and set off the wide grin which exposed two rows of well-set teeth.

Wayne's facial features, like Cal's, hinted at the Aleut Native heritage, but his blue eyes and brown hair betrayed the Scandinavian portion of his ancestry. Wayne was a fairly handsome fellow, and had been handy with the girls when younger, both local and outsider. But he had married a Kodiak girl and settled down, to first have a little girl and now a baby boy.

"Why you lookin' so down?" Wayne asked further, as he gave Cal a hearty slap on the shoulder. "Your girl giving you a bad time?" he grinned.

Cal glanced at him quickly but, concluding Wayne couldn't know about their troubles, lied: "Naw."

They walked on for a moment. However, the sudden urge to share his burden overwhelmed Cal, and he burst out: "Just having some trouble with my old man." He paused, then continued: "He's got it all planned out for me, what I'm supposed to do for the rest of my life, and he never even bothered to ask!" The freshness of the hurt still stung bitterly, and the anger in Cal's voice was easily read.

Wayne took it from there: "He wants you to go fishing all summer, crab all winter, then probably get your own boat, right?"

Cal whirled to face Wayne. "How did you know?" he demanded.

"Oh, word gets around. Your dad likes to brag on his family, you know," Wayne chuckled.

"But, you don't know if you want to do that, right?" he continued. "You think maybe you'd rather spend a year or so Outside, seeing the world—maybe even going to college and playing basketball?" He glanced over to look at Cal's face and, as he expected, surprise was written all over it. It was too much to contain, so Wayne broke down and howled with laughter.

Immediately, Cal's mood changed to one of insulted. "What the hell you laughing at?" he demanded angrily, and started to stomp off.

Wayne's firm hand gripped his arm tightly and pulled him back. Still laughing, he reassured Cal: "Hey, take it easy. I'm not laughing at you. It's just funny because the same thing happened to me! That's what I'm laughing at."

Cal's anger receded and he looked at Wayne. "You mean you weren't sure about what you wanted to do?"

"That's right, and I've found that happens to quite a few young guys. Not everybody, of course, because some guys just want to fish, and nothing else crosses their minds. Some, though, like you and me, we aren't sure. So, we think about maybe trying something else. As long as we just think about it, everything is okay—but when we actually try to do something, then the lid comes off!"

A rapid series of scenes, of the argument at home and his fight with Catherine, flooded through Cal's mind. "Yeah," he murmured, "I know what you mean."

The two of them started walking again, and turned off onto the beach, to sit on a log and look out at the waves rolling in from the horizon. The sound of the company diesel generator pulsed in the background, and the cries of gulls and crashing of the breakers filled the air. Cal threw a pebble at a group of nearby gulls and sent them screaming and cawing, as they rose in the air then back down, to jockey for positions on the tideline again.

"Look, let me tell you something," Wayne began: "when I was your age—even younger—there wasn't any high school here, or hardly even a grade school; we had to go out to a boarding school someplace. Not very many kids went out because... well, it's tough to leave home when you're only thirteen or younger." He paused. "I guess you gotta want to go. To be a little curious about what's goin' on out there—maybe even a little dissatisfied with life here."

He took a deep breath and continued: "Anyway, I was eager to go, because I had learned so many interesting things in school, about other places in Alaska and the rest of the world. But, at the same time, I was scared: I'd never been off the Chain before, and the biggest place I'd seen was Kodiak—and it was pretty small then, too. I went off anyway, though.

Maybe I was too dumb to know any better," he grinned, "but I went.

"For the first two years I went to Kodiak, 'cause it was closer, and I'd been there once before. Then, I went to Mount Edgecumbe High School in Sitka, down Southeast. It was a pretty big place for me, and I felt lost for a long time, but I gradually got into it. I played some basketball there, and we had a good team, too. Truthfully, there was too much to do, because my grades started slipping and I was lucky to graduate!" Wayne grinned broadly, as the memories flooded in.

"Anyway, I spent the summers back here fishing and, after I graduated, I was drafted and sent over to Vietnam. I was lucky because I worked in a supply office, doing bookkeeping and stuff; nobody ever shot at me. So, after I got out of the service, I came back here.

"My dad wanted me to fish again, and I tried it for a little while, but it just wasn't the same anymore. When I was a kid, the whole business was one big lark, nothing but fun. Sure, I worked hard, but it was a vacation compared to school. After the Army, though, it was just work. Just plain work." Wayne's voice trailed off, remembering.

"I could see right then that you either had to love those hard hours, and the cold and wet, facing the uncertainty of it all—'cause that's what it would always be—or you'd just get more and more bitter and hateful about it as the years went by, until you let the whole thing fall into a bottle of booze. I could see it happening to other young guys. I didn't love fishing like my dad did, but I wasn't going to be one of those broken, drunken bums I saw, either. So, I left.

"Holy, what a hullabaloo that raised!" he laughed, loudly. "My whole family thought I was crazy, for sure. But, I went to Anchorage, went to a community college for a year, to sharpen up my office skills, and held a job, too: I worked at a shipping agency, but it didn't last very long. Later on, I got a job with a Native corporation, gearing up to use the money they got from the Native Claims Settlement Act. But, that didn't work out, either."

Wayne paused, as if unsure about the next part. He threw a stone at the gulls, too, with the same result as Cal. "I had other things on my mind then, as well," he continued: "having trouble with my girl, I got to drinking a lot. I started missing work kind of often, and wasn't much good the rest of the time, because I was in a bad mood about my girl, and the inter-office fighting in the corporation. So, one day I just left and never went back—to my girl or the office. I came back here.

"Ho, I tell you, it was like walking into a fresh, hot shower and washing off all the dirt! I never felt so free and easy. No fighting at the office, no hassle with my girl, no more winding up at some party where I never knew a soul; at least now I knew who I was partying with!" Wayne chuckled and winked at Cal.

"Yeah, it was good. I was so eager to get out there fishin' and be my own boss, I 'bout drove everybody nuts. We had a pretty good year, and the next winter I married Ellen—met her when I was in school at Kodiak. Now I've got a family, house and a boat."

Cal had listened silently to Wayne's story, but now he asked: "You happy this way?"

"Yep!"

"You ever think about if things had been different, and you had settled Outside? In Alaska or down south?"

Wayne's assured smile slipped a little, and he leaned forward to pick up a pebble with strange markings on it. "Yeah, I think about that sometimes, like when I'm out fishin' late, and haven't got many fish in the hold. Sure, I think about the things I saw, the places I been, what I did… I think about all those things.

"But, let me tell ya, Cal," he dropped the rock and spoke seriously, "ya can't have it all: you can't live here and out there at the same time. And, once you leave here, comin' back won't be the same. The place here will change some while you're gone, but the biggest change will be in you; maybe you'll fit in okay, maybe you won't—that's the chance you're gonna take if you go out." Wayne glanced over at Cal. "You have to make a choice some time or other.

"But, I thought it would be good if you knew something about what can happen if you decide to go out. Some people can make it—I know guys from other villages that have and are going great—but then some people can't. I guess you gotta decide if you can, and if you want to take the chance." He continued to keep his eyes on Cal, then looked away.

A sudden gust of wind brought a chill to Cal.

They sat there for a few moments, silent, each buried in private thoughts. The waves crashed, the gulls continued their noisy forays and the generator engine thudded on.

Flying low above the horizon, a small, white speck grew larger and larger, as it neared the town, gradually assuming a bird-like form, but of a type created by mankind.

Since it was flying into the wind, the RAA Goose made a straight, head-on approach to the beach, throttled back engines as it settled into the water, then revved them up, to fight its way through the chop to the beach.

Cal spoke first: "Looks like we'll get mail today, after all."

Finally answering, Wayne added: "Yeah, I've got some engine parts coming. Hope they're aboard."

The plane was now at the beach, and roared its engines to ploddingly maneuver ashore. Then, the engines shut down and quiet reigned once again, as the mail pickup moved into position near the beach.

Out of habit, they rose and sauntered toward the plane, which was now unloading the green and orange mailbags. Just before reaching the circle of onlookers, Cal spoke:

"Say, uh, Wayne? Thanks for talkin' with me."

Wayne glanced over at Cal and their eyes met. "Well, I just thought maybe you'd like to know."

The words they exchanged weren't completely satisfying to either boy or man, since they each still felt a hunger for answers not yet met, but it was the best they could do. Both acted and spoke within the limits of their experience and self-image, and nothing more could be done or said.

After the plane was unloaded, the two nodded goodbye and went their separate ways.

24
Hunting

Paul

It was finally true spring weather when Paul's uncle came to take him hunting. The black brant geese were starting to flock on the flat marshlands of the Alaskan Peninsula, on the Bering Sea side, in preparation for the migration farther north, to traditional breeding and nesting areas. Caribou were still in rough shape from the winter, but they were fattening up. The cows were swollen with calves and were slowly foraging toward their accustomed calving grounds, farther up the Peninsula.

The tundra was bare below an elevation of 1,500 feet, but above that, the snow would hang on until the middle of June. Willows and alders clustering in stream bottoms were leafing out, and a profusion of tall grasses, wildflowers and salmonberry bushes were rapidly growing into the tangle of vegetation which appeared wherever the snow runoff trickled in a gully. On the open spaces between streams, the flowered, green carpet of tundra vegetation attempted to cover the volcanic rocks which formed the backbone of the hills.

Uncle James appeared unexpectedly one Saturday

morning, just as Paul was finishing breakfast. He was dressed for hunting and had two shotguns cradled in his right arm. Over one shoulder was slung a khaki canvas game bag, which Paul instantly recognized. Paul's immediate reaction to seeing James was first of scorn, from James's last drinking occasion, then excitement, because of the guns and game bag. It confused Paul to the point where he was unable to show either emotion, so he just sat there.

Stepping into the house, James was polite and subdued, greeting Julian and Mary cordially. He nodded to Paul and conversed with Julian for a minute or two. Paul relaxed as he realized his uncle was sober. Then, turning to Paul, James said: "Let's go huntin', boy."

Obeying the authority of habit, Paul started to get up, then halted as his confusion returned. Glancing at Julian and Mary for reassurance, he then jumped to his feet, grinning, "Sure!" and dashed off to his room for boots and coat. In a moment he reappeared, smiling and ready to go.

As they started out the door, Mary shoved a bag of smoked fish and some biscuits at Paul, who grinned sheepishly and stuffed them into a pocket. The screen door closed with a bang and they were off.

The two of them, with James's half-golden lab Snooker trotting ahead, set out down the lagoon road, then veered abruptly up a small valley to the northeast, down which a large stream rushed. Typical of Alaskan bush geography, this valley had a multitude of feeder streams, their narrow gullies choked with bushes and grass. The floor of the valley itself was similarly vegetated, except that the alders were larger and in big clumps, making it an ideal habitat for brown bears.

The man and boy followed the ancient bear trails along the stream banks, until the alders began to close in. They then struck out through the swampy grass to the clearer, heather-covered slopes of the encircling hills. Snooker eagerly ran from clump to clump, nose to the ground, investigating each fresh scent. Soon, they were halfway up the valley and near the beginning of an area where the alders grew in scattered, wind-flattened clumps, away from the bear trails. Not a word was spoken up to this point.

Now, James commented: "Thought you might want to shoot a few ptarmigan."

"Yeah, I do." Searching for something else to say, Paul added: "How long you been in town?" Talking with his uncle had never been easy.

Presently, James replied: "About two days." They crossed over a small tributary and climbed the gully bank. "I got fed up being over at home, so I just left. Nothing to do."

Snooker pointed a clump of bushes, and the two shifted their guns to the ready. Walking through the alders produced no birds, and they continued.

"Have you and Daddy been working on the nets?" Paul began again.

"Yeah, they're in good shape—ready to set, in fact, soon as the fish start running." They walked on toward more bushes. "I just got tired of getting stuff ready, and listening to your dad and Zeke and John argue and fight all the time. They been drinking some, every night for two weeks now. Jeez, the house is a mess: junk and bottles all over the place!" he scowled. "I had to get away."

A covey of ptarmigan, now almost entirely brown except for a few white patches, exploded in front of them, as Snooker flushed the birds. Immediately, two shots boomed out. Feathers flew and a body plummeted to the earth. Another shot, then another; more feathers gently floated down. With a whoop, Paul forged ahead while James quickly reloaded and closed in.

"Whir-r-r-r." A bird which had been hiding flew out from under James's feet, and he instantly shot it. Surprised and raising his head from having ducked down, Paul grinned back at his uncle. James reached down to pick up the bird. "Don't forget the ones that try to trick you. A good hunter keeps his gun loaded."

Paul picked up two birds and added them to James's trickster in the bag. Both reloaded and they set off again.

Throughout the morning, they worked the bushes on one side of the valley toward the stream head, flushing at least one bird from each alder patch. By the time they had reached the steep slope at the valley end, the two of them had bagged fourteen birds.

James sat down against a large tundra hummock and leaned back heavily against the soft carpet texture of its spongy surface. Paul set his load down and stepped over to the small stream, to get a drink. Where the water bounced down the gully, a small, shallow pool formed before it rushed on down another steep rocky fall.

Paul lay on his stomach and, placing his lips to the clear water, drank deeply until he felt he would burst. Wiping his lips as he rose, he sat next to James, leaned back and smiled broadly at the sky. It was great to be out again!

After a couple of minutes, James got up and took a drink at the stream. When he sat back down, he motioned to Paul's coat pocket: "How about a snack, eh?"

Paul had forgotten all about the fish and biscuits from Mary, and quickly dug them out. With nourishment satiating a momentarily forgotten hunger, both hunters felt more comfortable, and settled back to view the terrain they had crossed.

The sky was filled with flat, scudding clouds, which let broad shafts of sunlight through, to brighten up a portion of the valley and hillsides, speed through and disappear as the clouds converged. As such a beam of sunlight passed over them, Paul stretched out luxuriously on the soft tundra cover, growing sleepy as the sun warmed his face and clothing.

The sunlight also heated the vegetation, and aromas of purslane and saxifrage filled the air just above the ground, until the cooling breeze accompanying the clouds wafted it off. Small flying insects hummed in and out of this tiny tundra microcosm located so close to the ground's surface, and songbirds flitted about, feeding upon them.

It was a moment when time was suspended, and Paul felt at peace with himself and everyone. He felt that this flow of the natural order of life could envelope and carry him on forever. At last, he was outside hunting again. Slowly, his thoughts drifted and, half asleep, he imagined himself a great Aleut hunter, bringing home food for the survival of his family and village. Paul continued to conjure up a series of such images of himself, before he finally turned to James: "Uncle James?"

"Umm?"

"What was Grandpa like?" Paul's paternal grandfather had died when Paul was still small. "I mean, he went fishing and hunting a lot, didn't he?"

James pushed up the bill of his olive-green cap and, opening his eyelids halfway, looked at Paul. "Of course he did. What a dumb question! We all hunt and fish."

Rebuffed but determined to still pursue the matter, Paul continued: "Yeah, but did he do it all the time? Was that the only thing he did?"

James sat up a little now and looked closely at his nephew. Paul squirmed a little under the scrutiny. "You mean, did he have any other job? Work anyplace else?"

"Yeah, that's it," Paul shot back. "Did he?"

A thin smile appeared on James's bronzed, weathered face. "Sure, he had other jobs. He worked at the Unalaska salmon cannery for many years, and after that he was in the Army for a tour. Then, he set to fishing." James noted the disappointment which appeared on Paul's face. "Why? Don't you think he had to earn money? You can't just go out and live off the land, Paul; you gotta have money for supplies, like guns and ammunition, fuel, clothes and all that stuff. It takes money to live, Paul."

Paul was still confused. Something was wrong, but he couldn't quite figure it out. He tried again: "I thought Grandpa didn't go out and work for money. I thought he just hunted and fished for his family and the village. In school at

Ichinski they always told us that Aleuts used to just hunt and fish and live off the land, and that people lived well until the Russians and other white men came." He paused. "I thought Grandpa was a good Aleut hunter, and didn't work for anybody," he reflected, thoughtfully.

James broke the stillness with a rollicking laugh. Reaching over, he pulled Paul's cap down over his eyes. "Boy, they sure fed you a pile of garbage! If you knew only what those teachers told you in school, they'd have you believing that Aleuts just lived back in the Stone Age!" James rolled with laughter.

Presently, he exhausted his mirth and, seeing Paul's hurt expression, turned more serious. "Look, Paul, that's the way Aleuts used to live, but that was over two hundred years ago. That's all over."

He thought a moment, finally caught the drift of Paul's ideas, and continued: "Well, at least most of that kind of life is over and gone. A lot of people, like us, still need to hunt and fish, and we kind of live off the land. Some villages out farther do even more. But, we still hafta have money to buy things we need, and that means we gotta work at jobs that pay, like fishing commercially or at the cannery, or doing something someplace else. Grandpa worked Outside, your dad did and so did I."

"So, how come you aren't working out someplace else now, if you need money?"

"Well, because this is our home. I been out—went in the Navy, went to college and got a degree in accounting, worked in an office for a while, even learned to fly—but I came back, because… because this is where I belong. I feel good here."

James looked out at the valley spread before him. They could hear the sound of a stream in the distance, where it had grown large enough to develop a muffled roar. Somewhere above, a pair of winter wrens warbled out their songs.

25
Identity

Paul

Paul also listened as the wren songs drifted out over the hillsides. But his mind wasn't focused on life around him at the moment; he was struggling with the confusion of life, which churned within him.

After a short time, Paul replied, slowly: "I don't know, somehow it all seemed closer; that Grandpa lived like the Aleuts we were always told about at school—even by Grandma—and that he just hunted and fished all the time." He paused to throw a rock downhill at the stream. Looking up, he asked quietly: "What's an Aleut, anyway?"

Taken off guard, James didn't know how to answer. "What do you mean?"

"Well, I don't know. The people in Biorka say they're Aleuts but, holy, they live nothing like we do in Ichinski! The food they eat, how they dress, the way they act—none of it is like us. They got TV and electricity and stores… and lots of money. They don't even look Aleut, except for a few of 'em, but they say they're Aleut. I don't get it."

Once again, James looked deeply at Paul, in that same old penetrating way which always made Paul uneasy—except this time Paul would begin to understand a small part of its meaning.

"I'm an Aleut, you're an Aleut and the people at Ichinski are Aleuts. Some people at Biorka, like Moses and his family, are Aleut, too. But most of the rest of 'em, even though they say they are, aren't Aleut. It's more than them living different from us—that's part of it, but there's more to it. Of course, there's a lot of Russian and Scandinavian backgrounds in most of the families, but that's not most important. They don't think like us—that's the main thing."

He continued, after a pause: "They don't understand how to live out here—how to love the land and sea and rain, even though it sometimes can kill us. You gotta love it all, even though you're hurtin'... and that's what makes the difference between us."

"But, most of the kids and big people were born out here, too," Paul protested.

"Some of 'em were, sure," James replied, with a tight smile, "but many of 'em were actually born in some other place—Southeast, Anchorage, out west—and they lived there for a while, and eventually came back here. Some of 'em lived in some isolated spots out in the Bush, too, and things were tough, but it's not the same."

James looked out over the hills, to the sea beyond. "Unless each year you saw the salmon come fighting up these streams; lay for hours on your belly, watching a sow playing with her bear cubs; hunted seal out on the rocks; collected young salmonberry shoots in spring and dug rice roots in fall... all these things—unless you did 'em year after year, ever since you were a small kid, and still got a thrill out of it when you were grown up—you couldn't truly understand and love this place.

"Nobody can love this place, this country, except an Aleut. The Russians just wanted the sea otters and the Scandinavians wanted the money from fish. The white men from the lower forty-eight just want the salmon and crabs, and some hunting trophies to hang on their walls. And the government only wants a rock to put a weather station on, or lay out a military installation. But, who lives here, and loves this land, no matter what?" He paused dramatically, surprising himself at the emotion he showed, then continued: "Us real Aleuts, that's who.

Most of those people in town are just living like everybody else in the Lower 48, and the big Alaskan cities. They're all caught up in buying a lot of stuff they don't actually need. They've forgotten the Aleut way, and so they hafta work at jobs, making more and more money to keep their families and themselves happy. That means more and bigger boats, going Outside to get more schooling to learn a trade, working off away from home to earn more money, and being so lonely you drink up half of it."

He stopped, looked down at the twig he had been fiddling with, and seemed to struggle within himself about this—untypical for him—act of sharing thoughts.

He finally went on: "I know about this, Paul, 'cause I've tried working Outside, 'cause I thought I needed those things in stores and on TV I worked hard and bought a lot of stuff, but it didn't make me feel better. Tried acting like the white men and big city Natives, to be like 'em, but I never fit in. Tried sticking at a job long enough to move up and get a better position, but I got so homesick I ended up drinking too much and got fired." James chewed thoughtfully on the twig.

"I'm not proud of how I done. That's probably why I drank too much—still do. I wasn't happy not having those things, and not being able to act like a white man. And, at the same time, I wasn't happy being away from the land and sea I love, and eating good Aleut food, singing our songs and being a good, clean Aleut man. I was caught between two worlds, just like Grandpa, just like your dad, and just like all us people, all up and down the Peninsula and the Chain—just like you're caught, Paul." James eyed Paul intensely—the old piercing look.

"You're in the middle, too, and you hafta make up your mind what you're gonna be. In Biorka, and lots of other places where the white man's civilization is so strong, most of the people have made their choice and seem happy with that. They took the white man's way and stopped being Aleut, right here where it counts." He gently touched his chest.

"But, for some of 'em, it still hurts that they aren't true Aleuts. But they aren't white, either, and that hurts, too." James's voice cracked for a second. "Many try to drink their confusion away through booze, but it won't work. They don't know who they are, or where to go, or what to do. They try to buy the white man's way through mail-order catalogs and stuff at the stores, and this means they gotta work harder to earn money. This takes them away from the land and sea, away from the Aleut way—so, they drink more."

Uneasy, Paul stared at his uncle, who was having a tough time getting the words out—and with such emotion, too. But, he was nevertheless struck to his innermost roots by what the man had said.

"I know what I'm talking about, Paul." James's eyes clouded briefly, as he looked at Paul. "I've been through it, like lots of 'em. I fight it, and I get drunk sometimes, and I try to figure my way through it. Then, when I get frustrated, I drink too much again, and on it goes. But I'm still trying, Paul; I'm still trying, even though it maybe doesn't look like it."

He stopped pulling at the piece of tundra moss in front of him, and looked straight at Paul. "Your dad, now... he's given up. He just tries to wash it all away with booze. But I'm still trying. Ya gotta keep trying. If you don't, then you lose any Aleut you got left in you, and you just become part of a small, distorted copy of the white man's world: stuck way out in the Bush, depending on a Sears catalog to keep you alive.

"You're gonna have to face it, too," he looked at Paul, the boyish figure seeming to shrink back into the ground in fear, "now you're going to school down there." He pointed to the town below. "After that, you'll be thinking about going out to work, or more school. And, the more you get exposed to the Outside ways, the bigger chance you have of losing the Aleut in you."

"I won't go to school anymore, then," Paul blurted out.

"But, you gotta. You got no choice; it's the law. You gotta go to school."

"Then, I'll hide!"

"How you gonna hide, boy? You got nowhere to go.

Besides, that'd just make you a criminal."

"I could live off the land, hunting and fishing, like our people used to!" Paul argued back.

James smiled and shook his head, as he looked at Paul, his face now flushed with anger and pride, leaning forward tensely as if ready to spring instantly into flight—and freedom.

"I thought I told you, those days are gone. We don't know how to do or make all the things necessary for that, anymore. Sure, we know enough to help keep down the amount of cash we need, but it takes ten times that—a hundred times—to be able to live like our ancestors used to. You can't go back, Paul. None of us can go back... Nobody can ever go back."

Paul fell back, defeated. Tears welled in his eyes and his voice choked. "Well, what can I do? I'm Aleut. I know it because I feel it in me. I don't want to lose it."

James sighed deeply and looked at the beauty of the land about him. He turned to Paul. "I don't know, Paul; I haven't figured it out for myself, yet—maybe never will. But, I'm trying. Maybe... that's what you gotta remember: to keep trying." With a hint of confidence, he continued: "Learn what you can about the Outside and see what fits with what you feel, deep inside you. If it fits, use it to survive. If not, throw it as far away as you can. Watch out for the strings attached, too—you might get more than you asked for. That means you're gonna have a hard time putting off some things that look real good, and it's gonna hurt bad, but you gotta.

"Sometimes you'll meet people, Aleuts like us or Yupiks or other Natives down south—people of any minority—who seem to have some of the pieces to the puzzle. Carefully study what they say and do, and see if it fits for you, too. I've run into some people like that—really strong people, full of the way of the land and sea—who seem to be working it out. I tried to make it work for me, too, but it never fit good like I needed.

"The easiest way is to try to drink your troubles away, but it's no good: that only makes you feel worse about yourself, because you're just pouring the white man's crap right through your insides, and washing the real Aleut away. It's hard to fight, but it's the worst—I don't do so good on it, and I don't want you to let it get you. You hear?" James then gave Paul such a demonic, threatening stare that Paul believed if he should ever innocently touch even an empty bottle, James would instantly appear and beat him to a pulp.

James leaned back against the hillside and slumped. He looked as though every ounce of strength had drained out of him, since talking wasn't a strong point of comfort.

Both man and boy were silent for a while. Finally, James spoke again, somewhat detached and emotionless: "The Aleut is inside you, Paul. Look for it, know what it is and try to keep it. Understand how your heritage fits you in this big world you're facing. Then, you know who you are... and you'll be okay." He fell silent again, for some length of time.

Paul had almost decided that James had fallen asleep, when he suddenly got up, grabbed his gun and game bag, and started downhill. "Time to go," he announced, and set a fast pace back toward the lagoon and home.

Paul scrambled to get his gun and birds. Snooker had

instantly leaped to his feet from a dead sleep, and was already ahead of James, eagerly testing for scent.

It took a minute of hard walking to catch up to James and, when there, Paul glanced up at his uncle's stony face, eyes set straight ahead and unblinking. Paul directed his attention to the terrain and his footwork. The afternoon was well progressed, the sun almost reaching the hilltops, where it would soon disappear. A slight, cooling breeze was already streaming downhill, toward the valley bottom. It pushed them gently, yet resolutely, on their way toward home… and the future.

26
Transition

With the end of May, the school year drew to a close.

More than anything else, this event signaled the beginning of summer, since the seasonal changes in this part of the northern world were only gradations of more or less rain, wind and snow. In the middle of July, one could look around at the green tundra and leafy alders and conclude: yes, it is summer. The same could be said about January: that the snow on the hills and brown vegetation meant it was winter.

However, this was no guarantee that the weather would be appropriate to the calendar seasons, since it could sometimes be warmer and sunnier in January than in July; it was known to snow and turn quite cold in July, too. Therefore, aside from the migratory patterns of animals, the rhythm of human activity has always been the best definitive indicator of seasonal changes, and for many years that beacon of summer has been the closing of school.

For several weeks, Paul had been eagerly looking forward to his return to Ichinski. He was going to miss the few real friends he had made, especially Moses, but his vision of the return home blurred all such thoughts of regret. He was thrilled to be going, and it was all he could do to keep from daydreaming through classes, during the last weeks of school.

If any sad thought of leaving ever arose in Paul, it was one of pity for the other children of Biorka, who had to stay in town. They would never know the great life he led in Ichinski, spending his waking hours wandering the hillsides, catching spawning salmon, trapping parka squirrels, watching seals play offshore of Cape Dora, and growing a small vegetable garden on the sun-warmed bluff. All of these things the children of Biorka would never know. He felt sad about it, but such sadness was tempered by memories of the difficult times some of the children, especially the older ones, made for him.

Therefore, Paul was proud to be going on his journey—just as proud as other local kids would be, as they boarded the Goose for a trip to Anchorage, or to visit relatives down the Chain. As proud as other boys, when they set out with their fathers on their fishing vessels, for the first trip of the year.

Finally, the day after school was out, John Kristovich came over for supplies and to take Paul back.

As Paul carried his small bundle of baggage to the beach, on that sunny, windswept day, he felt as buoyant as the gulls which bobbed on the white-capped bay. He had a lofty spring to his step, and he felt as though the eyes of the entire town were on him.

Actually, there was a small crowd down at the beach, near where John's skiff was beached, but the crowd was grouped around the eight passengers, and pile of luggage and mail, which were soon to board the RAA plane parked at the water's edge. Five passengers were teachers leaving for the summer, and the others were locals, traveling to visit

Unalaska relatives. Goodbyes and well wishes were said, and baggage counted. The activity around the plane resembled that of bees about a solitary flower.

When Paul stepped into the small skiff and pushed off, he was sure that everyone had noticed his departure, and he reveled in the envy that he was sure his tormentors from school were now experiencing. He imagined that the children at the plane were now staring at his back, wishing with all of their hearts to be like Paul, and live the life of a true Aleut. He smiled to himself, as John opened the motor up and the boat leaped to the waves, sending the familiar smell of salty sea spray back into Paul's nose.

Of course, no one noticed the small figure clambering into the skiff, and jabbering with John as he struggled to get the outboard motor going. No one felt any emotion at all, as Paul sat in the bouncing bow of the receding boat, and relished the imagined victory of his leave-taking. The people on the beach belonged to another way of life, and the departure of a small boat returning to a village was of no consequence to them.

That night was the graduation ceremony. There were to have been five students graduating—the largest senior class yet, until Alice was murdered—but now Catherine, Ruth, Cal and Mark would make up the class. At the same ceremony would be nine eighth-graders, receiving their elementary school certificates. It was an event that was always highly attended, and this was the largest crowd of all.

On the gym bleachers sat the townspeople, habitually

bundled in coats, with small children seated on knees or being passed from relative to relative, to keep them entertained. The graduates were seated on folding chairs on the hardwood floor, facing a small stage, upon which sat—in excessive dignity—the superintendent, principal, school-board president and the guest speaker.

Little said that night was of much interest. Catherine (as class valedictorian) and Ruth (as salutatorian) managed to get through their two-minute speeches without breaking into tears or giggles, as had occurred in practice sessions, earlier. The superintendent expounded a few flowery phrases of congratulation, which made the students giggle, and told a couple of jokes no one understood. The guest speaker was a last-minute grab from the University of Alaska, who was passing through en route to another destination and, for some reason, talked about dwindling energy resources in the Lower 48, complete with charts too small for anyone to read. Students squirmed in their seats, small children chased around behind the bleachers, mothers shushed their babies and older adults struggled to stay awake.

However, it was soon over, everyone having survived the ordeal and glad to be out of the stuffy building.

Both Catherine and Cal had graduation parties at their houses that night, where family, relatives and friends came over to eat snacks, drink punch, congratulate the graduates and watch gifts being opened. Both parties were full of expressions of good fellowship and affection, as relatives and neighbors called up memories of times past, when the graduates were younger. This, in turn, brought about reflections upon their own past, and the things they did together.

Old photo albums were pored over, and new group portraits were requested and recorded, to the accompaniment of flashing bulbs and strobes. All the while, a continual stream of well-wishers passed through the doorway, sampling the well-supplied hors d'oeuvres table and stopping by to grasp the hand of the graduate, to welcome him or her to the status of adulthood.

By the time the last guests had left each household, it was late in the night. With awkward congratulations and goodnights from their parents, Cal and Catherine retired to their bedrooms, quite exhausted by the ordeal.

Yet, falling asleep was difficult that night—not because of the excitement of the day and evening, but because they were both numbed by the continual barrage of words and emotions concerning future expectations. It seemed as if everyone in the world was pushing them forward, to the brink of decision about their fate—an action they were not yet prepared to face.

27
Change

Catherine

Work on the new cannery was finally getting somewhere. A new concrete foundation was in, and structural steel beams for the walls and roof were going up. The dock was strengthened and pilings and decking replaced, enabling freighters to deposit building materials.

Most of the purse-seiners and gill-netters were gone, however, off to their fishing grounds, or unloading their catch at Nagai Pass, the closest operable Arctic Queen cannery. This was where Catherine was.

Faced with a lack of work in town this year, Catherine and many others went to live in the spartan dormitories of the Nagai Pass cannery, to continue working that summer. The work hours were just as long as the previous year, because the salmon run was just as good.

However, the cannery sheds were colder and not as well lit as the former cannery, at Biorka. The dormitory buildings were also not in very good shape, since they had not been used recently. So, some families just set up tents at a favorable location along the beach, and enjoyed the privacy afforded.

Despite these difficulties, the experience proved enjoyable

and profitable to most everyone. Fishermen got to see their families when they came to unload their catch and, for the women and children, it was somewhat of an adventure to be out where the demands were few and nature so close. During breaks, the workers could sit out on the beach or dock, and watch seals search amongst the pilings, looking for fallen fish. At noon, on nice days, they would often join their children for a brief picnic out on the tundra, for the lunch break. It had been five years since the cannery was operated, and the wildlife of the area was used to seeing only an occasional fishing boat passing by.

The area was also rich in clams and other forageable foods. As a result, everyone at the pass immensely enjoyed gathering wild food, in quantities which were no longer available in Biorka. For older persons, it brought back memories of times past. For the children, it was a chance to discover for themselves some of the ancient elements of the Aleut way of life.

Everything considered, the summer at Nagai Pass was a success, and would remain brightly etched in the participants' minds for years to come.

Like other Biorka townspeople, Catherine enjoyed her summer at the camp, with the freedom and closeness to nature that it allowed. But, she knew it was just a passing lark. She knew that no one would ever consider staying there past the fish run, no matter how much they now said they enjoyed it. Their idealization of "doing it like we used to" would fall aside once they got back to their gas stoves, television sets, washing machines, hairdryers and all the other paraphernalia of modern life.

Toward the last of August, Catherine caught a ride on a fishing vessel back to Biorka, to have a few weeks at home before she left for college. In June, she had received her acceptance papers from Sheldon Jackson College, in Sitka.

Ruth received hers at the same time, and had immediately rushed over, gushing with joy, to see Catherine. That night, their thoughts were all focused on what they believed would be the fun part of college.

Now, as the time to leave grew closer, Catherine's thoughts turned to the more serious and unknown aspects of going Outside. Where would she eat? How would she get around in Sitka? What if the schoolwork was too hard? What if she flunked? These questions continually diverted her attention and increasingly absorbed her thoughts, as time passed. When she saw Ruth, she would express her fears, but Ruth would wave them off. "We won't have a bit of trouble—you'll see," Ruth would encourage.

Although Catherine worried about going out, she wasn't about to change her mind once it was made up.

An aid in this decision was the recent marriage of her older sister, and the baby she bore that summer.

Her sister, Ada, had wanted nothing other than to get married, raise a family and live in Biorka for the rest of her life. She had gone with the same boy, Ross, throughout high school, and they had married the week after school was out last year.

Ada and Ross moved into a tiny house next to Catherine's family and settled in. Since that time, Catherine had watched her sister gradually letting her appearance go, gaining weight far over that which the growing baby added, and spending most of her day watching TV or drinking coffee with other young, married women. The house was always a mess, and Ada didn't seem to have anything to say to Catherine, except about the big plans she and Ross had made, and the accumulating details of her pregnancy.

When the baby boy was born, things didn't get much better, as far as Catherine could see. Ada didn't lose any of her excess weight, and the baby's mess only added to the confusion of housekeeping. She also now carried her baby along to visit her friends, and all she could talk about were the details of his feeding, sleeping and bowel movements. Catherine was thoroughly disgusted with the changes in her sister.

Even more disturbing was the way she saw Ada slip into the typical fisherman's wife role, which most other young women of the town assumed. Although she knew it didn't have to be that way, it seemed inevitable that they all ended up with similar concerns and activities, reinforcing her earlier worries about what kind of life was ahead for her, in Biorka.

Yet, the security offered by the role was attractive. It meant fewer decisions to be made, and definite certainty of her future. She was both attracted and repulsed—a tough position to be in. Confused, she felt justified in leaving it all for a while; maybe she would be able to think more clearly later.

Coming back from the post office one day, she ran into Cal. They had seen very little of each other that summer, except for an occasional chat at the unloading dock in Nagai Pass, when her noon hour coincided with the *Panof* discharging its load of fish. Then, they were still not over their falling-out of the past spring.

This time, they talked about Catherine's coming departure, and she noticed a change in Cal: he seemed less defensive, and had dropped some of the cocky mannerisms which were his trademark as a basketball star. She was heartened, yet suspicious of this change.

"I thought you applied to go to Fairbanks," Catherine offhandedly inquired, after they had talked about her departure date and other plans.

Instead of scuffing his feet on the ground and remaining silent, as he normally would, Cal shifted his weight to the other foot and looked up at her, his arms remaining folded on his chest.

"Yeah, I did," he softly admitted. "I don't know why. Maybe just to get back at my dad for making all those plans without asking me." He was silent for a moment. "Maybe I just wanted to see if Coach Irving was right: that I was good enough to play ball in college. I dunno. I get pretty confused about it all."

Catherine looked incredulously at him. *Cal admitting he's having problems?* Hopefully, but cautiously, she asked: "Is that why you never could talk to me, way back when?"

"Yeah, I guess so. I was just so mixed up I couldn't talk about it." He looked at Catherine. "I guess I made it kinda tough on you." His eyes met hers, but she said nothing and looked away.

Presently, she asked: "What are you going to do now?"

This was very hard for Cal, and he almost walked away, though Catherine never knew it. He swallowed hard. "Oh, I'll keep on fishing through the season, I guess." *As if I have a choice,* he added, in his mind.

"And, this fall?"

"Well, I guess we're gonna get a crab boat from Homer, to bring up here. Me, Dad and Uncle Walter will crab through the season; finish up sometime in February. Should be pretty good, too; each year has been better than the last. I figure I'll make a good bundle from my part of the crew share." He grinned upon thinking about the money he'd be able to save. Then, slightly embarrassed at his apparent enthusiasm, he grew more somber.

"And then?"

It seemed to Cal that her questions, and the decisions they brought boiling to the surface, would never cease. Feeling somewhat trapped, Cal's temper began to rise, and he replied, abruptly: "Hell, I don't know." Struggling with his frustration, he continued: "I suppose I'll fish. Maybe I'll go to Seattle, or maybe I'll… just do nothing." He was silent for a moment, then, in a lowered voice, concluded: "It all depends,

I guess."

"On what, Cal?"

"On the fish, the weather... how I feel about... you."

With these last words, Catherine's face softened and a smile broke out. Hesitating at first, she reached out and lightly put her hand on one of Cal's folded arms.

"That's all we can do, Cal: wait and see what happens—to you, to me, to everything around us. That's all we can do. A year is a long time; maybe, by then, we'll know what we're doing, and whether we'll each be doing it alone... or together."

Cal looked down at the hand on his arm, gently lifted his left hand and grasped hers in his. They started to walk along the boardwalk together.

"Yeah, it's a long time, but I guess we can write, huh?" And his face broke into his usual consuming grin.

Catherine giggled and teasingly bumped against his shoulder, coming to stay there, walking close to him.

28
Takeoff

Catherine

Two weeks later, Catherine was hurrying toward the landing spot on the beach, carrying a large shoulder bag. Ahead, her father had already reached the beach with the two large suitcases he was carrying, while her mother walked beside her with a smaller one.

As was the customary procedure, the RAA pilot radioed the post office as soon as he took off from the nearby airport. The postmaster then sent out a phone call to Biorka homes that had passengers waiting to catch the plane—and the rush was on.

Catherine had packed the night before, since no one ever knew exactly when the plane would radio its takeoff, because of the fluky weather, and it was necessary to be ready for departure at any time. Consequently, she was ready and waiting.

As she and her mother walked down the boardwalk, they didn't talk much. Her mother would add a few words of advice and encouragement—already repeated many times that morning—then fall silent.

Catherine thought very little about anything, which

surprised her somewhat. She concluded that she had done everything which needed doing, and said everything necessary to everyone, so what was left to think about? She was sick of trying to imagine what the future would hold! So, as the two of them walked silently, side by side, Catherine thought of her mother, and how she must feel to see her daughter leave. She tried to put herself in her mother's place, but the effort failed; she hardly knew what her own place was, let alone her mother's.

Nearing the landing spot, Catherine saw that a small crowd of onlookers was present, standing in groups, idly chatting, and occasionally scanning the horizon for the plane. Some of her high-school friends were there—other passengers, some relatives—and Cal with some friends, standing off to the side. He raised his hand in a wave and grinned. She waved a quick flick of the wrist and smiled, then turned away.

These elements of the scene were minor, however, because what grabbed her attention was what she saw next: sitting on a large suitcase, with others piled next to her on the beach, was Ruth. But, it was a Ruth that Catherine could hardly recognize. Instead of the sparkling, bright-eyed, buoyant bubble Catherine had always known, sat this withered, ashen-faced gnome of a girl, surrounded by two very worried parents. Catherine was so startled by the ghostly appearance of her friend when she first saw her, that she stumbled on a beach rock.

Setting her bags down with the rest of the luggage, Catherine rushed over to her. "Ruth! What's the matter! Are you sick?"

Ruth said nothing, but sat looking straight ahead, tears welling in her eyes. Getting no response, Catherine looked up questioningly at Ruth's parents.

"She was fine until we got down here a few moments ago," Ruth's mother explained, "then she just sat down on that suitcase and started to tremble and cry. I don't know what's wrong."

Catherine looked down at her friend. "Ruth?" No answer. She bent closer and looked her in the face. "Ruth, what's the matter?"

Slowly, Ruth unfroze her stare and looked up at Catherine, her eyes open wide and rimmed with tears. Catherine had never seen a face so drained of color before. Ruth's entire body trembled slightly.

"What is it, Ruth?"

Her voice quivering, Ruth whispered, hoarsely: "I can't."

Just then, someone called out, "There it is!" and the crowd's attention was riveted on the horizon.

Barely visible, but growing larger by the second, the Goose made a broad turn around the jutting headland and leveled out, straight for the beach. Now it was possible to hear the familiar raspy drone of its engines.

Catherine turned back to Ruth. "You can't what?"

"I can't go. I just can't!" Ruth declared, through upwelling tears.

"You don't want to?" Catherine was having a great deal of difficulty absorbing what was happening. "I thought you—"

"I *do* want to," Ruth threw back, "but… then… I don't. I

don't know what I want." Ruth broke down in sobs. "I'm scared." Her voice shook so badly, through the tears and sobs, it was difficult to understand her words.

Catherine stood there in shock. She couldn't believe it. Ruth was the one who'd had the idea first, and was always pushing her to go. *Now look at her! What am I supposed to do?* Catherine's mind raced.

By now, the Goose had landed in the water. Within a minute, it growled its way onto the shore and lurched to a halt. A moment after the propellers stopped, the back hatch was flung open and the pilot's head emerged.

As he hurled out the mailbags, he shouted: "Let's get moving, folks. There's a thirty-knot wind due here in twenty minutes, and I want to be out to sea before then."

The pilot's words and the sound of concern in his voice had an immediate effect upon the crowd: without hesitation, several men rushed forward to grab the mailbags off the beach and carry them to the postmaster's pickup truck. At the same time, other men started hauling outbound bags off of the pickup, and handing them up for the pilot to stow inside. Another hatch was opened, and luggage was handed up to a man standing on the wing. The passengers began to quickly say their goodbyes and head for the plane.

Amidst this bustle of activity, Ruth sat on her bags and Catherine stood before her.

With the din of preparations ringing in her head, Catherine struggled to comprehend the consequences of her alternatives. She could go, of course, but who would she room with or, for that matter, have as a companion? If she stayed, *then* where would she be? Her mind brought forth images that had contributed to the original decision she had made.

Did she truly need Ruth to go? Yet, what made her think that she *didn't* need Ruth?

And, Cal? Would staying change their relationship? *But that's already been settled, hasn't it? What if…?*

"Catherine," her mother's quiet, firm voice broke in, "they're ready to leave. I've already put your bags aboard."

Catherine whirled around and, for a brief instant their eyes met, and held with a depth of affection and understanding that had not passed between them for many years. She carelessly flung herself into her mother's arms and, with her head buried on her mother's shoulder and tears flowing down her cheeks, Catherine whispered: "Thank you, Momma. Thank you." Her decision was made for her—perhaps one of the last major parental decisions her mother would ever make.

Catherine turned to hug and kiss Ruth. "We'll write, Ruth, and maybe semester break you can come, okay?"

Ruth tried her best to smile through her tears and nod.

After a respectful peck on her father's cheek, and a hug in his big arms, she turned straight to the plane and climbed in.

Her memory of the next few moments was blurred, by the rapid sequence of events which quickly found her a thousand feet above the water, and taking her last look at the seemingly miniature town below, as the plane banked to head out to sea.

Goodbye, she thought, mistily. *Goodbye to everything. And, hello to… what?*

She didn't know *what*—and couldn't be concerned at the

moment, because the promised thirty-knot gale was beginning to buffet the plane hard, making it difficult to do anything but concentrate on keeping her breakfast down.

29
Decision

Paul

Paul was again perched on the topmost craggy peak of his favorite mountain. He had found a niche in the rocks, which sheltered him against the buffeting winds of that overcast day. Occasionally, the sun would lazily burn through the clouds, enough to warm his face and clothing, making it pleasant to be away from the work at home and out on his own again.

As he watched the pageantry of daytime wear upon the distant vistas of sea, mountains and village, Paul's thoughts gradually fell to rambling over the brief months of summer vacation which came and went, and left Paul more perilously balanced on the brink of decision than before.

He spent most of the time fishing with his dad and uncle, beach-seining salmon with their skiff. The long hours and days of setting, clearing and stacking the net brought less time for the carefree summer playtime Paul had expected.

Once, when complaining of aching arm and back muscles, his father reprimanded him for his childish behavior. "You're gettin' older now, Paul. You gotta forget about actin' like a kid."

At first, Paul was pleased to be considered more grown up, but as the days of work wore by and grew more monotonous, he fervently wished that he could be out there with Willie and Mary, playing on the beach, rather than straining against the wet net, befouled with seaweed and rotting, spawned-out salmon. However, while the extended work did not have the attraction of play, Paul was drawn to some level of satisfaction at definitely learning more of what it meant to be an Aleut fisherman, working to support his family and village.

He was able to go to Nagai Pass twice, when the village men took large loads of salmon there, on one of the bigger fishing boats. However, with the cannery located farther away this summer, it was much more difficult to sell salmon. As a result, a larger proportion of the fish taken that summer was put up on tall, outdoor racks to dry, for a winter food supply. As a result, when he wasn't out fishing, much of the rest of Paul's time was taken up repairing drying racks, stoking smoke-shed fires, cleaning and splitting fish, and taking care of the fish when dried.

Once, impressed with the amount of fish they were storing, Paul asked his grandmother if this was about how many fish they dried in the "olden days". She chuckled loudly, as she hung up another split salmon. "Lord, no, boy! We put up ten times this."

Stunned, Paul asked: "But, that meant about all you did was catch fish, clean 'em, hang 'em up and start all over again!"

"That's right," she declared, flatly. "We had to live on

those fish year-round."

This revelation tarnished Paul's image of the carefree life of his ancestors, as he imagined it. Considering this, and the hard work of netting enough fish to sell at the cannery, Paul gradually concluded that a village fisherman's life wasn't quite as he had pictured it.

Another unpleasantness was the drinking that went on in the village. While in Biorka, he hadn't been around much heavy drinking. Although Julian and Mary both sometimes drank, it was more controlled in their house. If anybody showed up drunk and Julian hadn't been drinking himself, he would escort them off to the bar, and stay with them there a while. Paul never knew why that pattern was this way in the Golodoff household, since it was not the same in all Biorka homes, but he was thankful that's what they did. As a result, when he returned to Ichinski, he was a little unprepared for the occasional heavy drinking right in the house where he lived, and the mess and arguing that went along with it. He had temporarily forgotten this upsetting part of village life.

So, when things got out of hand, Paul would fall back into his old habit and slip off to one of his hiding places, to wait the night out. Numerous times that summer, as he was scrunched up behind some old barrels in a storage shed, Paul would reflect that at least in Biorka it was easier and more comfortable to avoid this kind of thing.

That summer, too, John Kristovich had moved his family to Biorka; he, his wife and son Freddie were living with his younger brother, Dan, until he could get a house located for his family. John said he knew that their leaving would make it harder on those who stayed, but he argued that he just couldn't stay any longer. It wasn't the same as when his parents and grandparents had lived there. At that time, he reminisced, there were lots of people they could share successes and failures with. That way, nobody suffered greatly from the effects of living in such an isolated place, and you could enjoy the bonds of friendship and family relationship which necessarily developed. Besides, in those days, people didn't feel they needed much cash. They bought some grocery staples, tools and clothing at Biorka (and Sandpoint before that), where they also sold their salmon, but they required little else.

Now, it was all different, John maintained, and people felt they needed more money to buy things. Almost everybody had moved to Biorka or elsewhere in search of work, or to be closer to the cannery. "What future is there in staying?" he asked.

With the Kristovichs gone, the Andreanofs and Millers began to talk of moving on, too, maybe next year.

Amidst the continual discussion about the Kristovichs' move, and the idea of others moving, Paul's childhood vision of being a noble Aleut hunter, forever stalking the hills and seas of his beloved Ichinski, dulled yet even further.

He rarely ever focused his attention directly upon the problem in its entirety. But now, as he sat nestled amongst the rocks of his mountain, the consequences of his summer experiences and resultant reality check couldn't be put off. If he could no longer look forward to spending his life in Ichinski, as he had spent the last thirteen years, then what?

The only other life he knew was the one he had led at Biorka. He had never fit in well there, but it was the only other choice he knew. He was aware that other places of escape existed—like Kodiak and Anchorage—but these were still too scary and vague to be considered. Perhaps later on, but not now.

So, what were his choices? He could return to school in Biorka and, despite the difficulties and being homesick, prepare himself for a new life. But, this also meant risking the loss of his Aleut heritage, as James had warned. Or, he could stay in Ichinski, avoiding the law and the outside world, becoming increasingly more dependent upon traditional Aleut subsistence techniques, as the village became deserted. But this only postponed things; after everybody left, then what? Where could he go?

The thinking was too much for him. How could he possibly sort it out?

Slowly, the words of Uncle James; the hard work keeping the drying racks full; the disappointment of his return to Ichinski; and the growing attraction of life Outside all flooded into Paul's mind and, like a swelling wave crashing upon a littered shore, washed clear the debris of his thoughts. Paul finally knew what he must do.

His body was shaking noticeably as he shivered from the cold, and Paul realized that he had been sitting in his rock niche for too long. He hadn't noticed the discomfort of the chill, since the agony of his thinking had been so overpowering. But now, with the finality of a decision made, it roused his awareness.

Lovingly, Paul took a last, sweeping look at his precious mountains, tundra and sea. He then slipped down between the horns of the Devil and started home. In a few days, he would leave for Biorka.

But, first, he had some more playing to do.

30
Acceptance

Paul

The morning broke to fair skies, not completely overcast, with only a brisk chop on the bay, brought by a light wind playing about the rounded shoreline, where Ichinski lay. Although his father had said nothing directly to him, Paul knew that today was the day he would leave for Biorka and school.

Being older now, and certainly more experienced, he had learned to interpret the clues better: adults talking more secretively the last two nights, his father being excessively outgoing with him, and acting embarrassed when Paul asked what the extra gas can in the skiff was for. He would not be taken unaware this time.

The previous night he had packed a cardboard box with the best of his chapel hand-me-down clothing, folding each item as neatly as he could. He even added a couple of his favorite possessions, which had always been kept in Ichinski: a small fox trap, a flat, round drum and beater, and a harmonica—all gifts from his grandfather. He looked thoughtfully at each item, as he put it in the box and carefully nestled it amongst his meager clothing supply.

James and his father had earlier that morning gone outside

the house, to uncover the skiff and mount the motor on the transom, all the while talking to each other, as they glanced at the sky and the wind patterns, playing farther out to sea.

Paul had made it a point to eat breakfast early and be ready when they came back into the house. After the two men had eaten, his father called out: "Hey, Paul?"

Paul stepped into the room, his coat on and cap in hand. "Yes, Dad?"

"I've, uh, gotta go..." and he stopped short. His eyes traveled down from Paul's face to the cardboard box, so neatly tied with knotted string of three different sizes, and tightly gripped under his arm. He looked back up at Paul and, shifting his eyes away, finished his message: "Time to go, boy."

Paul pulled his knit cap over his ears and went to the door. "Bye, Grandma," he called, as he went outside.

The tang of the salt air and fresh beach odors tingled Paul's nose, and he took a deep breath. He loved this air, which never stood still, and always held remembrances of a past day's storm and rain. It seemed to him that the air was always moving and vibrant, as if it were a living thing itself, existing only to test those who ventured into its path, and to reward those who survived and saw the beauty.

He glanced about at the crashing waves upon the beach, the screaming, fighting gulls wheeling overhead, the distant vistas of cone-shaped, snowy peaks, freshly thrown up from the Earth by a great volcanic hand—all belonging with the penetrating air which made them alive, and part of the whole which was this place of his youth and love. A place that, even now, as he stood on the threshold of leaving once again, he was convinced could never be completely erased from his memory and feelings. It was too strong to be easily removed.

Reassured that the transience of his life lay in the short journey he was about to make, and not in the existence of the place about him, Paul stepped willingly toward the waiting skiff.

James and Dick caught up with Paul by the time he reached the boat. Silently, the three set about getting it down to the water's edge and arranging their gear aboard. As they worked, Dick noticed that his son wasn't wearing his usual hip boots and patched rain gear; instead, he had on a pair of brown Oxfords, some checkered wash-pants and a brown shirt. The wind blew Paul's now tattered red coat about his body. The whipping garment revealed a lankier, more solid body than Dick remembered. Why, he was even taller, too; standing next to James, Paul's head was almost to James's shoulder.

James had noticed the difference, too, but had not cast the significance merely in the frame of "growing up", as his brother had. For many years, he had watched his nephew closely, to see if he could detect a spark of insight which might be kindled—a maturity which would enable the boy to find a path through the morass of cultural conflict which loomed ahead.

He tightened the motor down on the stern and paused. Perhaps Paul could find the route that he and his brother had failed to. As it is the universal hope of all humanity, that in their progeny lies the promise of their salvation, so too James was at this moment looking at Paul, weighing the chances that this small boy might break out of the conflict binding his past and present, and find a path between the two worlds. Yes, Paul looked different, as he stood waiting for the skiff to be launched, but would these changes lead to success or failure?

James threw Paul a rain slicker. "You better get goin'."

Paul pulled the slicker on, since he knew the trip would be wet going over, and glanced at his uncle. There it was, as always: that same questioning look. This time, though, it didn't seem so threatening. *Well, I guess I'll get used to it someday,* Paul concluded, and turned his attention to the more pressing matter at hand.

By the time the boat was loaded and ready, the last few feet of bare sand and rock were already encroached upon by the rising tide, and the boat lifted and bounced with each rushing wave.

"You get up, Paul," his father ordered; "you ain't got your boots on." Paul complied and sat in the bow, holding onto the gunwales.

"Now!" The two men shoved hard with the rising wave, and the skiff was free. James continued to push, as Dick jumped aboard and pulled the starter cord. As the motor caught and the boat pulled away from the shore, James stood silently in the light surf, water swirling over the knee-patches on his hip boots.

He watched for a few moments, as the skiff carrying the man and boy began pointing into heavier waves. Finally, without looking back, he turned and walked straight up the beach, toward the small group of houses.

Paul watched his uncle from the now speeding boat. Quickly, James's figure merged with the gentle shape of the shoreline and sweep of the hills, until his outline was no longer distinct.

Paul then turned to his father, sitting at the stern—outboard engine handle in one strong hand, the other tightly gripping the gunwale, to brace himself against the pounding of the waves. Spray blew over the bow, and his father would duck just in time to miss each one.

Whitecaps danced over the rolling surface of the bay, and gulls screeched raucously over the roar of the outboard. A rain squall could be seen driving down over the hills, and it would be upon them in a few minutes. To the left, closer now, big combers from the open sea were breaking in frothy explosions, upon the jagged rocks off Cape Dora.

An oddly angled wave suddenly caught Dick off-guard, and drenched him thoroughly with spray. Wiping a forearm across his face to clear his eyes, he looked forward at the young man, hunched up under the protective canvas of the bow. With a broad grin wrinkling his face from ear to ear, he shouted: "Fine day, eh?"

Paul looked at the dripping, comical, weather-beaten face of this open, simple man who was his father. And, gripping the gunwales tightly, he grinned back just as broadly and openly, letting the roar of the motor and the sea swallow their laughter.

About the Author

Lance V. Packer was born on a farm in eastern Washington state. He grew up immersed in a close relationship with that world of structured nature, and had the time and freedom to think and wonder about what he observed about himself, during the expansionist times of American life after World War Two.

He was a youthful sponge, absorbing everything newly discovered—from ants underfoot, to distant, glaciated, volcanic peaks, to the attraction of the wiles of young girls with flashing eyes. All were approached enthusiastically, and sought further exploration and questioning.

Years of further life adventures—including Peace Corps service, a Ph.D. in anthropology, and twenty-seven years teaching public school in Alaska—broadened that youthful experience. That is the bedrock upon which this book is written.

Please share your thoughts and questions at the author's blog, forum and website: https://www.lancepacker.com.

Also, posting your honest review at Amazon.com can help spur other potential readers to consider the book: https://www.amazon.com/Caught-Between-Worlds-Lance-Packer/dp/1737006502

Thank you.